THE PRESIDENT AND ME:

George Washington AND THE MAGIC HAT

Deborah Kalb

Schiffer Publishing Ltd

4880 Lower Valley Road • Atglen, PA 19310

Other Schiffer Books for Middle Grade Readers:
Freestyle, Monica S. Baker, 978-0-7643-3538-9

Grandfather's Secret, Lois Szymanski, Illustrated by Kelli Nash,
   978-0-7643-3535-8

Leonard Calvert and the Maryland Adventure, Ann Jensen,
   Illustrated by Marcy Dunn Ramsey, 978-0-7643-3685-0

Published by Schiffer Publishing, Ltd.
4880 Lower Valley Road
Atglen, PA 19310
Phone: (610) 593-1777; Fax: (610) 593-2002
E-mail: Info@schifferbooks.com
Web: www.schifferbooks.com
Copyright © 2016 by Deborah Kalb

Library of Congress Control Number: 2015939119
Designed by RoS
Cover design by Brenda McCallum
Type set in Bookman Old Style
ISBN: 978-0-7643-5110-5
Printed in The United States of America

For our complete selection of fine books on this and related subjects, please visit our website at www.schifferbooks.com. You may also write for a free catalog.

Schiffer Publishing's titles are available at special discounts for bulk purchases for sales promotions or premiums. Special editions, including personalized covers, corporate imprints, and excerpts can be created in large quantities for special needs. For more information, contact the publisher.

We are always looking for people to write books on new and related subjects. If you have an idea for a book, please contact us at proposals@schifferbooks.com.

Dedication

To my parents, Marvin and Madeleine Kalb—
always an inspiration.

Chapter
~1~

Sam had no idea when that particular Thursday morning began that a few hours later he would end up back in the eighteenth century almost trampled by George Washington and his horse.

For all Sam knew, it was going to be just another ordinary day. Well, not completely ordinary—field trips were always kind of exciting. Ms. Martin, his teacher, was enthusiastically herding Sam's fifth-grade class out of the school and onto the bus. "Mount Vernon, here we come!" she cried, causing a few of the noisier boys to start chanting, "Here we come! Here we come!"

Out of habit, Sam looked around for Andrew, his former best friend. The two of them had always sat together on field trips, ever since their trip to the US Capitol way back in kindergarten. But of course Andrew was with Ryan and Tom, his new best friends from the baseball travel team.

Sam sighed. He watched as Andrew, Ryan, and Tom squashed themselves, all three together, into a seat. Sam found a seat a few rows in back of them. It's okay, he told himself reassuringly. It's more fun to have the whole seat to myself, anyway. I get all this extra room.

He watched as everyone else settled into their seats, including the parent chaperones, and, feeling a little self-conscious, noted that he was almost the only person sitting by himself. No one was sitting next to Oliver, either. But Oliver, characteristically, seemed not to care about his solitary state. And no one seemed to notice that Sam, or Oliver, was unaccompanied and friendless. They were all too busy talking, laughing, and enjoying themselves.

Ms. Martin charged down the aisle, holding her clipboard. Glancing around, she spotted the empty spot next to Sam and plopped down into it, exhaling. She caught her breath and turned to Sam, her eyes gleaming. "Sam!" she exclaimed. "This is going to be great!" Sam muttered that yes, indeed, it was going to be great.

Ms. Martin was wearing her dark blue Eastview Elementary School shirt that the teachers always wore on field trips, but she had accessorized it with a red, white, and blue beaded necklace and a pin bearing the likeness of George Washington. Dangling earrings shaped like tiny replicas of the White House nestled in her curly gray hair. "Of course, George Washington never actually lived in the White House," Ms. Martin said, apparently sensing that Sam had noticed her earrings. "John Adams was the first president to move in there."

Sam nodded. They had been studying the Revolutionary War period for several weeks now, since the beginning of the school year, and this trip to Mount Vernon, George Washington's home, was the highlight of the unit, along with a play about George Washington that Sam's class

was to perform the following week. Sam had hoped to get the part of George Washington, but instead, to everyone's surprise, it had gone to Oliver. Sam was assigned to play one of a group of soldiers.

Sam's school was in Bethesda, Maryland, and the ride to Mount Vernon, in Alexandria, Virginia, would take about forty-five minutes. Ms. Martin had gone over all the details in class the day before. They would go on a tour of the house, look through the museum, eat in the cafeteria, and then each of them would be able to buy something at the gift shop, assuming it was okay with their parents.

Sam's mom had given him some money that morning. "I'm so sorry I can't come along this time," she had said, giving Sam a hug goodbye. "You know how much I love going along on your field trips." She did, Sam knew.

But she was filling in that week for one of the news anchorwomen at the TV station, so it just wasn't possible. And Sam's dad was away at a conference.

So here he was, sitting with Ms. Martin. "George Washington just couldn't wait to get back to Mount Vernon," Ms. Martin was saying. "Every time he had to leave, whether it was to command the army or serve as president, he really wanted to come back. And when he finally retired, then he died two years later, poor thing. He and Martha didn't have that long to just relax and enjoy themselves at Mount Vernon."

Sam nodded again. Sometimes it was hard to get a word in when Ms. Martin was excited about some particular topic. "He wasn't just a military leader and a political leader, though, Sam, he also was a farmer. And he most likely designed Mount Vernon himself." Ms. Martin clasped her hands and smiled at Sam. "How amazing!"

Sam agreed. George Washington did seem like an amazing guy. Almost too amazing. Too perfect. Had he ever done anything wrong in his life? Sam wondered what it would have been like to hang out with George Washington. Did George ever think things were funny, or was he totally serious all the time? Having to run the army, and then the country, must have been a lot of work. He tried to imagine George, coming back after a long, difficult military campaign, laughing and joking around, but he couldn't. He tried to picture George smiling, and couldn't quite manage that, either. Didn't he have wooden teeth? No, Ms. Martin had told them that wasn't true. But whatever they were made of, maybe they just didn't look so good, and maybe that was why he didn't smile very much.

The bus had left Maryland and was well into Virginia by this point, progressing down a parkway lined with leafy trees. Some of the kids in the back were laughing and pointing to the second bus, behind them, which held the other two fifth-grade classes. Ava, Sam's across-the-street neighbor, and her best friend Samantha, in the seat behind Sam, were giggling about something and whispering to each other. The two of them were always whispering secrets back and forth.

Often, they'd be sitting on the swing on Ava's front porch, and when Sam's cousin, Nigel, who was in college and lived with Sam's family, would show up, the giggling and whispering would get even more intense. Apparently, they thought Nigel was incredibly cool. Nigel was from London, and his English accent made him seem even more fascinating.

Sam had talked about George Washington and the Revolutionary War quite a lot with Nigel. After all, the colonists had been rebelling against Great Britain, trying to free themselves from British rule, so Nigel, living in England, had grown up learning about the war from a different perspective. But now he was in college at none other than George Washington University in Washington, DC, studying history, and he knew a lot more than Sam did about the whole thing.

With a loud squeal of the brakes, the bus pulled into a parking space. Ms. Martin sprang from her seat next to Sam and began directing everyone off the bus and into the orientation center for the start of the tour.

Mount Vernon, Sam learned, as the class toured the house and continued up a pathway to the nearby museum, had belonged to George's older half-brother, Lawrence Washington, and when he died it had passed to George. George had expanded the house over the years, first adding more of a second floor, and then adding new wings on either side.

By the time the fifth-graders got to the cafeteria, everyone was worn out and hungry. Sam found himself sitting with Oliver. Andrew was a few tables away with Ryan and Tom. It was as if he and Andrew had never been best friends, Sam reflected, had never sat together in the cafeteria every day, had never spent most of their afternoons playing in the neighborhood park.

Sam had always been on the same Little League team with Andrew. Neither of them had been very good, but they weren't awful either. Well, to be honest, Andrew had always been better than Sam. For one thing, Andrew was older than Sam. Sam had just turned ten last month, in August, and Andrew would already be turning eleven in a couple of days. Maybe that gave Andrew a little bit of an advantage. Or at least that's what Sam had always told himself.

Then about a year ago, Andrew had decided that he wanted to be good at baseball. He had signed up for baseball camps and some special baseball clinics. Of course, he had asked Sam if he wanted to do it, too, because the two of them had always done everything together, since they had first met at the park when they were babies.

But Sam had said no. He didn't really want to spend that much time on baseball. He was in a couple of school plays, and he was in the chess club, and he wanted to have some time to just hang out and ride his bike around the neighborhood, now that his parents had finally let him do that unsupervised by them or Nigel.

Now, looking back at how things had developed, he wished he had joined Andrew. Because Andrew had gotten really good at baseball, good enough that he made it onto the travel team with Ryan and Tom, two kids who had always been good at baseball and who had been on the travel team for a while already. And now Andrew didn't hang out with Sam any more, because Andrew was always busy with baseball. And Sam missed him.

"George Washington was really the only person who could lead the country," Oliver was droning, as he took a large bite of his cheese pizza.

"That's probably true," Sam said politely.

Oliver had come to Eastview toward the end of fourth grade. He hadn't really made any friends, because he acted as if he thought he was better than all the other kids. Smarter, too. Oliver probably was some sort of genius, Sam thought glumly.

Oddly enough, Sam was one of the only kids that Oliver would speak to. Maybe because they were in the chess club together, or because Sam lived nearby, just a couple of blocks away, and they both got off the school bus at the bus stop near the playground every day.

"It's been a real challenge trying to capture his essence for the school play," Oliver continued, waving his piece of pizza in the air and spraying crumbs from his mouth as he talked. "I really see myself as somewhat similar to him in terms of our strategic minds, but it still takes some work to get into character."

And that was the other thing about Oliver: he was kind of clueless. Pretty much everyone knew that Sam had expected to get the part of George Washington, because he usually got one of the big parts in the class plays, except when it involved a lot of singing. Singing wasn't Sam's strong point. But he really loved being on stage, even though he was a little shy otherwise.

Oliver, however, seemed to have no idea that maybe going on and on to Sam about playing George Washington might sort of hurt Sam's feelings. And no one else seemed to have any idea why Oliver had gotten the part. Even Andrew had broken away momentarily from Ryan and Tom to sidle over to Sam, punch him lightly on the arm, and say he was sorry Sam hadn't been picked as George. That meant a lot to Sam.

Still, at least sitting with Oliver, however annoying he was, meant that Sam didn't have to sit by himself. Ms. Martin, who had been at a nearby table with Ava and Samantha and a couple of other girls, now jumped up and clapped her hands to get everyone's attention. "Class, please finish up and follow me over to the gift shop," she proclaimed.

There was a general flurry as the fifth-graders gathered up their trash, threw it out, and got into a ragged line behind Ms. Martin. The gift shop was just down the hall from the cafeteria, and they all followed her inside. "Fifteen minutes," she called. "I will be here by the door, and then once you've all paid for your souvenirs, we'll be getting back onto the bus."

The gift shop was enormous, and was filled with souvenirs featuring the likeness of George Washington. "I think I'll get a couple of books," Oliver announced, and disappeared toward some shelves of Washington biographies. Sam heaved a sigh of relief.

Ava and Samantha were exclaiming over a pile of small plush horses. "Oh, I just have to get one of these," Ava was gushing. "Absolutely," Samantha agreed.

Sam found himself pulled toward a round metal rack filled with tricornered hats, the black type he'd seen in so many pictures of colonists. Is this what he wanted to get? There were some cool-looking gadgets in the other direction, binoculars and other things.

Sam began to head toward the binoculars, but found that he couldn't move in their direction. It was as if there were an invisible wall between Sam and the binoculars, and he couldn't break through it. Instead, he found his arm reaching toward the hats.

But I don't want a hat, he said to himself. I want a set of binoculars! His hand, however, seemed to have other ideas. It reached, not just for the hat at the top, but for one several hats down. It looked older than the others, which were all crisp and new.

As Sam's hand, moving apparently of its own accord, reached toward the old-looking hat, he felt a shock like

electricity run through his entire body. He pulled his hand back sharply.

Once again, he tried to turn toward the shelf where the binoculars lay. But once again, his hand found its way toward the hat, toward that particular old, tattered-looking hat.

He pulled the hat out of the pile, and, to his surprise, it leaped onto his head. All at once, the room whirled around, making Sam feel dizzy. He closed his eyes.

When he opened them, the gift shop wasn't there. Instead, he was standing outside on a huge lawn, looking toward Mount Vernon. But the house looked different. Smaller somehow.

Sam heard what sounded like a horse coming up behind him, and turned around. He almost collapsed. There was George Washington, riding toward him. Sam stared, not believing what he was seeing. This is just a dream, he told himself. This isn't really happening. George drew closer and closer as Sam remained in place, transfixed, the hat firmly planted on his head.

"Good day, young sir," George Washington said to Sam, doffing his hat, and he proceeded on toward the house. Sam realized he should have taken off his own hat as a gesture of respect, and he belatedly did so. At once, he found himself back in the gift shop, quivering from head to toe.

"Sam, you were in a total trance," Samantha was saying, waving both hands in front of Sam's face. She and Ava were standing in front of him, smirking. "Come on! Ms. Martin said we only have two more minutes before we have to get back on the bus!"

"Okay," Sam managed to say. What had just happened? His mom would probably say he needed to get a better night's sleep. His dad, a scientist, would probably scoff and say that the whole thing was just a figment of Sam's often-overactive imagination. Nigel would probably be the best one to talk to about this.

Sam tried to put the hat back on the top of the pile and make his way toward the binoculars, but instead found himself, tattered hat in hand, at the cash register. The cashier smiled at Sam as she took his money and put the hat into a paper bag with the Mount Vernon logo on it. "Please come back and visit us again soon!"

Sam nodded, not sure what was going on. He hadn't meant to buy the hat, had he?

Back on the bus, Sam ended up sitting by himself. Ms. Martin had taken a seat next to Oliver this time, who once again didn't have any other kids to sit with either. The bus ride was bumpy, and as the passengers squealed, Sam heard an angry snorting sound coming from inside the Mount Vernon shopping bag.

"My stars, what sort of conveyance is this?" came a querulous, somewhat high-pitched voice. "What horse creates such giant bumps? On which road do we travel?" Sam shook his head. Was he hearing things now, as well as seeing things? He must have been imagining it. He looked around. No one else seemed to have heard anything out of the ordinary. Andrew was a few rows back with Ryan and Tom, deep in a discussion about something. Probably the Nationals' latest game. Ms. Martin seemed in the throes of conversation with Oliver. Probably about George Washington's strategic mind.

"Well, child?" said the voice. "Do you not answer when your elders speak to you?" Sam frowned. This was really getting weirder and weirder. Should he look inside the bag? No, that was just giving in to whatever strange hallucination he seemed to be in the middle of. "Really!" said the voice, sounding angry, but also a little hurt. "The impudence!"

Well, all right. Sam peered into the Mount Vernon bag, glancing around to see if anyone else was paying attention. But no one was. "At last!" the voice said. It seemed to be coming from the hat. "I asked you a question! What horse creates such giant bumps? This is a most uncomfortable ride!" Indeed, the bus jolted and bumped again, causing shrieks of glee from various kids.

"No, it's not a horse, it's a bus," said Sam, trying to explain. "And yes, it can be kind of bumpy."

"A bus?" said the hat, for that was indeed what was speaking. "And what might that be?"

"It's like a car, but bigger," Sam said. "With a motor. It's not a horse. Although cars do have horsepower, I think."

"Humph," snorted the hat. "A car? Horsepower? Please remove me from this bag at once, so I can cast a glance at my surroundings!" Sam complied, removing the hat from the bag.

"Well?" the hat said, sounding impatient. "Are you not a boy? Do you not wear a hat?"

"A baseball hat, sometimes," Sam said. "You know. But we're not supposed to wear hats at school."

"Not wear hats at school?" said the hat, sounding confused. "And what is this base ball of which you speak? Please put me on your head so I can see around me! I can see nothing from here on your lap!"

Sam sighed. Really, this hat was kind of bossy. And what would happen if he put it on again? Would he be back out in the field near Mount Vernon?

"Hi, boy!" said the hat. "Did I not ask you to place me upon your head, so that I could see more clearly?"

Sam reluctantly did so. To his relief, he remained seated on the bus. "Okay?" he asked the hat. "Now can you see?"

A huge gasp came from the vicinity of Sam's head. "Aieeeeee!" screamed the hat. "Aieeeeee! Where am I? What is this? We are moving more quickly than a team of horses could pull General Washington's carriage! More quickly than General Washington himself could ride, and he is the best horseman in the colony!"

Sam was grateful that the bus was so noisy that no one could hear this stream of conversation from the hat. It would have been hard to explain.

"Love the hat," said Samantha, tapping Sam on the shoulder from the seat behind him and causing Sam to jump. "Ava and I got these really cute T-shirts, and little plush horses that come with them, see?" And she pulled a yellow Mount Vernon T-shirt and a brown plush horse out of her bag.

"Nice," Sam said, nodding.

"Well, I'm glad someone seems to love me," the hat said approvingly, seeming to have calmed down from its fright of a minute before. "What a pleasant, gentle young lady!"

"Um," Sam began. He wasn't so sure he'd describe Samantha as pleasant and gentle. He remembered that back in first grade, some of the kids, struck by the similarities in the names "Sam" and "Samantha," had started up that annoying chant, "Sam and Samantha, sitting in a tree, k-i-s-s-i-n-g." Sam had gotten really upset, and Andrew had stepped in and told the other kids to stop it. Samantha, meanwhile, had smiled, enjoying the attention. Every so often, if someone wanted to get Sam upset, they'd call him "Samantha."

"Can I try it on?" Samantha asked.

"Yeah, let us try it on, okay?" Ava chimed in.

"I just don't think that would be a good idea," Sam said. Maybe the hat would whisk Samantha and/or Ava back to the eighteenth century, as it seemed to have done with Sam in the gift shop. Of course, now it was on Sam's head and it wasn't whisking him anywhere. And maybe it wouldn't be such a bad thing to have Ava and Samantha off in the eighteenth century for a while. But then he'd have to explain to Ava's mom, his across-the-street neighbor whom he'd known since he was really little, what had happened to Ava, and that might be difficult.

"Pish," said the hat, reprovingly. "Please do let the young gentleladies have a turn. Although I would imagine they would look more fetching in a bonnet. But the world has turned upside down, and I find myself in a strange conveyance, so why not throw all convention to the winds! I find myself traveling far from home, in more ways than one."

Sam was somewhat confused by what the hat was saying, but he handed it over to Samantha, who giggled and put it on. To Sam's relief, or at least, partial relief, Samantha was still sitting in the seat behind him. No trips back to George Washington's time for her.

She handed the hat to Ava, who jammed the hat on her head but also remained firmly in place on the seat of the bus.

So what had happened back there in the gift shop, Sam asked himself. Had he just imagined the whole thing? One time when he was a lot younger, he had imagined that he was in a sequel to the *Star Wars* movies, and it had all become so vivid that he couldn't tell what had really happened. Andrew had convinced him that it was all imaginary, but Sam was never entirely sure.

As Ava handed the hat back to Sam, the bus pulled up in the bus circle in front of Eastview, and Ms. Martin hustled everyone off the bus and back into the classroom.

Sam, who had shoved the hat back into the Mount Vernon bag, was just sitting down at his desk when the hat started complaining again. "Be this a classroom?" it said. "It is so bright! What are those dreadful bright glowing things yonder?" And it hopped up and down in the bag, as if to gesture at the fluorescent ceiling lights.

"I'll explain later," Sam whispered. He was starting to understand. The hat must really be from George Washington's time! That's why it looked so old and tattered, nothing like the replicas that surrounded it in the gift shop. But how had it gotten into a modern-day gift shop in the first place? And how had it chosen Sam to buy it and take it with him? What did it want Sam to do, anyway? Would he get to go back to George Washington's time again?

Chapter ~2~

"I don't understand," Nigel said. He and Sam were in the family room having a snack, and Nigel's long legs were stretched across the yellow-flowered sofa. Sam curled up in the nearby armchair, the Mount Vernon bag with the hat in his lap. "You actually saw George Washington? Riding up to you on a horse?" Nigel looked skeptical.

As well he might, Sam reflected. He had managed to get the hat home on the bus after school without any further complaints on the hat's part, but now the hat was giving Sam the silent treatment.

"Really," Sam said. "It really did happen. It's just that now the hat's probably in a bad mood or something, and it's not talking."

"Cracker?" Nigel offered, holding the box out to Sam, who took a handful. "Well," Nigel continued, "perhaps it just doesn't like me. Perhaps it harbors resentment toward me because I'm from London."

"Tory," the hat muttered from within the bag, coming to life. "Traitor. Benedict Arnold."

Nigel leaped about a foot in the air. "What?" he spluttered. "Who said that?"

"It's the hat," Sam said. "I think you got its attention."

"Did it really say that?" Nigel said, sounding a little shaky and looking a little green. "Did it actually talk?"

"Yes," Sam said patiently. "That's what I've been trying to tell you for the past hour or so. It talks! And I did go back in time, I know it!"

Nigel sat down again on the sofa, his complexion slowly returning to normal. He took a deep breath. "All right," he said to the hat. "Tell us a little about yourself, then."

"Please," the hat said frostily. "Speak not to me, traitor."

"I'm not a traitor," Nigel protested. "Yes, I am British, but I'm from the twenty-first century! I'm a student! I study history at G. W."

"Twenty-first century?" the hat said. "Is that where I am? Oh, bother. Now how on earth did that happen?" It paused. "And what do you mean, G. W.? Is that an appropriate way to speak of the general?"

"George Washington University," Nigel explained more respectfully. "It was named after the general."

"Ah," the hat said, sounding more pleased. "Of course. And now I will take another rest. All this traveling is making me very tired."

Tired? Sam thought. But he needed to prove to Nigel that his trip to the eighteenth century really had happened. If the hat was too tired, then maybe that would be it and there would be no more trips. Or maybe Sam had just imagined it all? He had to do something.

"Oh, come on," Sam cajoled, taking the hat out of the Mount Vernon bag. "Don't you want to take me on another adventure? And you can bring my cousin along, too." He put the hat on his head, but nothing happened. He was still sitting with Nigel in the family room, the box of crackers on the table.

"Let me have a go," Nigel said, taking the hat off Sam's head and putting it on his own. Still, nothing happened.

"I told you, I'm tired," the hat said peevishly. "I need to rest. And I'm still not quite sure about you," it continued, seeming to gesture toward Nigel. "Friend or foe?"

"Oh, definitely friend," Nigel said. "But if you're tired, then please do take a rest." He took the hat off and put it back in the bag, which seemed to serve as a sort of cocoon, or nest, for the hat.

Sam, though frustrated, realized there was no point in arguing with the hat right now. "All right," he said. "Fine. I think I'll just go for a bike ride."

"Brilliant," Nigel said. "I'll be in my room if you need me." And he disappeared into his room in the basement.

Sam headed to the garage, put his helmet on, and wheeled his bike out. But before he could get on it, he spotted Ava on her porch swing across the street, a book in her lap. He waved, and she beckoned him over.

"You want to ride around?" Sam asked, wheeling the bike across the street. He always used to ride with Andrew, but these days, Andrew was always at baseball practice, or traveling off to a game.

"No, I need to finish this book and write my book report by tomorrow," Ava said. "I guess I waited a little too long to get started. It's about Abigail Adams. Samantha's doing hers on Martha Washington."

"Oh?" Sam said. Maybe if the hat would wake up and take him on another weird adventure, he'd get to meet Martha, too. She seemed a little more approachable than George. Maybe she'd invite him to a meal at Mount Vernon. That would be fun. He pictured the five of them— George, Martha, their two grandchildren, whom he'd learned about on the Mount Vernon tour, and himself, sitting at a table in the Mount Vernon family dining room, which, he remembered, had really bright green walls. Maybe the grandchildren would teach him some eighteenth-century games. Didn't they roll hoops around back then? He figured that couldn't be too hard.

"So he just really, really gets on my nerves," Ava was saying. "Are you listening to me at all, Sam?"

"Yes, of course," Sam said. He hadn't been, but he knew perfectly well who Ava was complaining about: J. P., her stepbrother. Ava's mom had gotten remarried last year, and Ava's new stepdad and his son had moved into Ava's house. J. P. was in third grade. He went back and forth on different days between Ava's house and his mom's house, which was somewhere not too far away.

Actually, Sam kind of liked J. P. He was bilingual in English and French, which was cool. His real name was Jean-Pierre, but almost no one except J. P.'s mom, who was French, called him that. But Ava couldn't stand him.

"And everyone thinks he's so cute," Ava was continuing. "So they give him extra pieces of cake, or extra little presents, or whatever. I mean, the other day he got this whole Lego® set from my mom's best friend. And what did she give me?"

"Nothing?" Sam ventured.

"Well, not exactly nothing. She gave me a couple of pairs of socks. But it wasn't really the same kind of thing as a whole big Lego set."

"Is J. P. around today?" Sam asked. Honestly, he'd rather hang out with J. P. than listen to Ava complain any more.

"No, he's with his mom," Ava said. "Thank goodness. Anyway, I'd better get back to this book—I still have a few more chapters to read."

"Okay," Sam said. And he started to get on his bike. But then he remembered the hat. So maybe it was tired. But maybe it would like a ride around the neighborhood. A little fresh air never hurt anyone. And it was a really nice day outside.

He went back home and threw the hat, which had awakened and was grumbling and protesting, into his backpack, which he put on, and he rushed out and got back on the bike.

"What? Now what kind of contraption have you put me into?" the hat demanded.

Sam pedaled quickly past a few more houses before he responded. He didn't want Ava to see him apparently talking to himself.

"It's a backpack," Sam said. "To carry my things to school and back. You know, books, papers, folders."

"A back pack," the hat mused. "Yes, yes. A useful sort of thing, eh? Perhaps some of the general's men would like to try one. Now, pray tell, where are we? What sort of area is this?"

They were approaching the neighborhood park, which featured a small bike trail. Sam pedaled onto the trail. "This is a park," he said. "To play in, ride bikes in, you know."

"Yes, sounds very nice," the hat said. "May I take a look?"

That's right, Sam realized. The hat wasn't really getting to enjoy the day, all cooped up in the backpack. "Sure," he said. "Sorry about that." And he got off the bike near a picnic table, sat down, and retrieved the hat from the backpack. "There you go," he said, taking off the bike helmet and putting the hat on his head.

All at once, the dizzy feeling came over Sam again, causing him to lean over and put his head into his lap. The world seemed to swirl around and around, until everything stopped. Sam lifted his head. He was sitting on a tree stump. Mount Vernon, in its smaller incarnation, was ahead of him, and a tall figure was walking toward him across the lawn.

Sam peered over at the figure. It was male but didn't seem to be an adult. Maybe a teenager?

"Good day," the young man said, approaching Sam, who could tell that the young man was extremely tall. "Are you a visitor to Mount Vernon? It's my brother's home."

"Your brother?" Sam said, feeling dazed. This teenager must be George! "I mean, good day to you, too. Yes, I'm visiting."

"From which parts do you travel?" the young man asked.

"Bethesda, Maryland," Sam replied. "I'm Sam."

"Oh, Maryland!" the young man said. "You've come a far distance." He looked around him. "But where is your horse? Or did you come by carriage? Or cart?"

"Um," Sam answered, not entirely sure what the right answer should be. Telling the truth—that he had come by grumpy magic hat—was clearly not an option.

But, fortunately, the young man spoke again. "I apologize, I haven't introduced myself. I'm George. George Washington."

"Yes, you are," Sam managed to say. "But how old are you?"

"I'm fifteen," George said. "And you?"

"Only ten," Sam answered, standing up from the tree stump and gazing up at George, who still towered over him. "You're really tall."

"Yes, I know," said George. "Lawrence says I'll probably grow some more. And I'm hoping I'll be heading out to sea very soon, now that I'm almost grown."

"To sea?" Sam was confused. George Washington had been in the army, not the navy, right?

"I'm trying to talk my mother into sending me to sea," George confided. "I really do think a sailor's life's for me.

She's been reluctant, although I think I may have convinced her to allow me to do it. My father died several years ago, and she doesn't want me to be too far away."

"Well, that makes sense, I guess," Sam said. His head was still spinning somewhat, and he wasn't thinking too clearly. Here he was talking to the first president of the United States! Could this really be happening? And shouldn't he be taking advantage of this opportunity to ask George some incredible questions?

"What really happened with that cherry tree, anyway?" Sam blurted out. "I mean, did you cut it down or not? Or was that whole story made up?"

"Cherry tree?" George looked puzzled. "I'm afraid I don't know what you're referring to."

"When you were younger?" Sam persisted. "Maybe about my age? And you chopped down a cherry tree, and then confessed it to your father because you couldn't tell a lie?"

"Hmmm," George said, wrinkling his brow. "No, I'm sorry, I don't remember anything like that. Maybe you're thinking of one of my cousins? Or one of my brothers?"

"Maybe," Sam said. That cherry tree story must be just a fable, then.

"I'm riding over to Ferry Farm now," George said. "To see my mother and prepare to pack up for my time at sea. It's quite a long ride to Ferry Farm, but would you care to come along? Perhaps your horse is in the stable?" And he gestured toward a nearby outbuilding.

"No, I didn't come on a horse," Sam said. "But I'd like to come along." Meeting George's mother would be interesting.

"Oh, well, we can borrow one of Lawrence's horses, then," George said hospitably.

Sam squirmed. He had never been on a horse, except for pony rides when he was younger. But he wasn't sure how to tell George, who clearly was an expert horseman.

"You do ride?" George asked.

"Well, actually, no," Sam said.

George looked incredulous, but his good manners prevailed. "Well, then, you'll ride with me." And he walked Sam over to the stable, where a beautiful chestnut horse was waiting. George lifted Sam up onto the horse and jumped up behind him, and the two of them were off, riding like the wind.

All thoughts of trying to converse with George flew out of Sam's head. All he could think of was hanging on for dear life as George steered the horse up winding trails and through wooded paths. It seemed like hours. At last, the horse slowed down as George pulled firmly on the reins, and a small house appeared in a clearing.

"This is where my mother lives," George explained as Sam caught his breath. "She'll no doubt be glad to see me as I've stayed for quite a number of weeks at Mount Vernon with Lawrence."

Lawrence, Sam remembered, was George's older half-brother. And George had a lot of younger siblings, too, a few of whom rushed out to greet him. Along with them came a careworn-looking woman. She didn't seem especially pleased to see George.

"Mother!" George cried, dismounting and helping Sam off the horse. Sam found that his legs were wobbly. "And Betty! And John!"

"George, my son," Mrs. Washington said, giving her oldest son a quick peck on the cheek.

"Well, Mother, I am planning to pack my trunks and preparing to go to sea," George said excitedly, ruffling the hair of one of his younger brothers.

"George, a letter has come just this day from my brother in London," Mrs. Washington said. "He is very much opposed to your going to sea and believes you should stay here and help me and the younger children. Money is always short, as you know."

"But Mother!" George pleaded. "This cannot be! You had almost given your consent!"

"You are still not of the age of majority," Mrs. Washington said. "And I had not given my consent, not entirely. I was waiting to hear from your uncle. And now I have. So that is final." And she headed back into the house, the younger children following her inside.

"But that's not right!" George protested, starting to rush after his mother. "I had my heart set on a career at sea!"

Poor George Washington! Sam knew how it felt to have your parent deny you something you really wanted. Like the time he had wanted to go to the Nationals game with Andrew and his family and sit in some special fancy seats and meet some of the players. He had been looking forward to it for months, but Sam's parents had insisted that he go with them to a distant cousin's bat mitzvah instead. And Sam didn't even know the bat mitzvah girl, anyway. How could he make George feel better?

"Wait," Sam said, putting his hand on George's arm. "Maybe a career on land would be better suited to your talents." Hadn't George also worked as a surveyor as a young man? "Have you considered surveying?"

"Oh, yes, I have begun some work in that area," George said, stopping in his tracks. "I do enjoy it."

"One day, you could become a great general," Sam continued, warming to his task. He felt as if he were back on stage at Eastview, in a starring role. "You could command the armies of the American colonies against the British. You could become a household name, the most famous man in the colonies!" Seeing that he had captured George's attention, he kept talking. "You could become the very first president of the United States!"

"Against the British?" George said, sounding confused. "But we are British!"

"Well, right now you are," Sam said. Maybe he should stop. He didn't want to confuse George any further. "Anyway, you could have a really fantastic career without going to sea. That's my point."

George paused, a thoughtful look on his face. "Yes, Sam, perhaps you are right. Perhaps I should look at this as what was meant to be."

"Yes," Sam said. "I do think this is what's meant to be." His head itched, and he pulled the hat off to scratch.

To his dismay, all of a sudden he was sitting back on the bench in the neighborhood park. George was nowhere in sight.

"But . . ." Sam said, looking at the hat in his hand. He hadn't been able to continue talking with George. He had wanted to meet some of the younger kids, who looked closer to his age. And, while George's mother didn't seem all that sympathetic a figure, it would have been worthwhile to ask her some questions about what George was like as a boy.

"You removed me from your head," the hat said reprovingly. "That's the rule—I need to stay firmly affixed to your head, else you will return to your own time in the so-called twenty-first century."

"So-called?" Sam said. "It really is the twenty-first century!"

The hat snorted. "Whatever you say," it said. "But that's the rule. And now this travel has made me tired. I must rest."

"Will I get to go back?" Sam asked frantically. "I want to talk to George some more. Maybe see him when he's a little older."

"You'll find out," said the hat. "Now put me back in the backpack so I can take a nap." Sam did, and soon a gentle snoring sound emanated from the backpack.

Chapter

~3~

"And then there's the old story about the cherry tree," Ms. Martin was saying, writing "Cherry Tree" on the classroom whiteboard with a red marker. "True or false?"

"Father, I cannot tell a lie," Oliver pronounced, without raising his hand. "I chopped down that little cherry tree."

Sam's hand shot into the air. "False," he called out. "I mean, George couldn't remember anything about that story, so that kind of proves it, doesn't it?"

☐ True ☐ False

Ava, whose desk was next to Sam's, and Samantha, a few desks away, started tittering. "Oh, really, Sam? Did George tell you that himself?" Ava whispered, loud enough for the whole class to hear. A few other kids, including Ryan and Tom, started laughing. Sam felt himself turning red. What had he said?

"Well, Sam just has a good imagination," Ms. Martin said, winking at Sam. "Settle down, everyone. But Sam's probably right about the cherry tree. Here's another question for you." Under "Cherry Tree," she wrote "Sailor."

"Did George Washington want to be a sailor at some point, or was the army always his goal?"

Again, Sam was the first to raise his hand. "Yes, he did want to be a sailor. When he was a teenager. But his mom told him he couldn't." He remembered the stern Mrs. Washington. "I don't think she was very nice, really."

"Very good, Sam," said Ms. Martin approvingly. "You've been doing your homework, I see!"

It was the day after Sam's adventure with George and Mrs. Washington, and the hat had been more or less dormant except for a few grumbles from inside its bag, where Sam had put it for the night.

In the morning, it was still apparently sleeping, so Sam left it alone and headed to school. At least today was Friday, which meant the weekend was near, and Sam hoped that the hat would be ready by then for another adventure.

He had, of course, filled Nigel in on the afternoon's events. The two of them had decided that telling Sam's parents (his father was due back from his business trip that evening) about the hat's magical abilities was completely unnecessary.

"Okay," Ms. Martin said, concluding the history lesson. "And now it's time for a special announcement."

Oh, no. Amidst the excitement of meeting George, Sam had almost forgotten what was coming: tomorrow, Saturday, was Andrew's birthday.

Most years, Sam had looked forward excitedly to Andrew's birthday. As Andrew's acknowledged best friend, Sam generally got the best seat at the party, right next to Andrew, and sometimes even got to help cut the cake.

This year was different. In fact, he wondered why Andrew had even bothered to invite him to his party. Probably his parents had made him do it.

But when Sam had suggested to his mom that he just stay home, she had been very much opposed. "I know you and Andrew haven't been as close lately, sweetie," she had said, putting a comforting arm around Sam, "but you've been friends for so long. I really think you should go. If only for old times' sake." Sam's dad had concurred.

"Andrew's birthday is tomorrow!" Ms. Martin was saying happily, as various kids called out birthday greetings to Andrew. "So let's all sing." And the class started in on "Happy Birthday," Ryan and Tom singing extra-loud and Andrew looking a little embarrassed but happy nonetheless. Sam sang along, but an empty feeling was creeping in. How would he ever find another best friend?

The empty feeling dogged Sam all the way home from school, and he told his parents that he wanted to go to bed early that night, right after dinner. The hat was no help, snoring away in its bag. Sam wondered if it had abandoned him, too.

The next morning dawned chilly and rainy. Not a good morning for riding his bike or for much of anything else, except worrying about the party, which started at 2:00 that afternoon. Andrew's parents were taking a group of his friends to see the latest adventure movie, and then they would all have pizza at Andrew's house.

Sam got some homework done, and just before 2:00, he resignedly picked up the gift he'd gotten for Andrew (a heavy volume about baseball) and trudged the two blocks to Andrew's house.

He could always hang out with Andrew's little sister, anyway. So what if she was only five and in kindergarten? At least she would talk to him.

The familiar blue door to Andrew's house opened, and Andrew's father patted Sam on the back. "Sam, buddy! How have you been? All the guys are hanging out down in the basement before we head out to the movie. You know the way." And Andrew's dad gave a chuckle.

Of course Sam knew the way. He knew every inch of Andrew's house, from the one worn spot on the upstairs hallway carpeting to the faint stain on the basement wall from the time he and Andrew had had a food fight when they were in first grade (and had gotten in big trouble for it).

"Sam! How tall you are!" Sam's mom was at the head of the stairs to the basement, and she gave Sam a big hug. Sam handed her the gift, which she put in a pile on a table near the doorway. "Elizabeth is so excited to see you!"

Andrew's little sister, her hair in two pigtails, rushed up the stairs, tackled Sam, and started to tickle him. "Sammy!" she yelled. "I missed you! Let's play the tickle game!"

Sam found himself almost about to cry. He had missed being over at Andrew's house. It had been months since he'd been there. He saw Elizabeth at school occasionally, but he figured it probably wasn't a good idea to tickle her at school, much to her disappointment. After tickling Elizabeth for a few minutes, Sam noticed all the voices coming from the basement, and his heart sank.

"Come on, Sammy!" Elizabeth cried, grabbing Sam's arm and pulling him down the steps to the basement.

Sam looked around. There was Andrew, of course, and there, naturally, were Ryan and Tom, plus a few other boys who also were on their baseball team. They all gave half-hearted waves and returned to their conversation, except Andrew.

"Happy birthday, Andrew," Sam said.

"Hey, thanks," Andrew said.

Neither of them looked at the other.

"Sammy, let me show you my gerbil," Elizabeth shrilled, much to Sam's relief. "He lives down here." And she took Sam's hand and directed him to a cage in the corner.

Sam occupied himself with Elizabeth and the gerbil until it was time to leave for the movie, and during the movie he didn't have to talk to anyone (although Ryan and Tom spent most of the movie poking Andrew, who sat between them, and whispering comments to him).

Sam sat between Andrew's mom and Elizabeth, who proclaimed that she wasn't scared of anything in the movie, although Sam didn't entirely believe her. Elizabeth pretty much monopolized Sam during the pizza dinner back at Andrew's house, and once "Happy Birthday" was sung once more and cake was eaten, Sam said his thanks and made his way home.

His parents had gone out for an early dinner, and Nigel was waiting for him. "So?" Nigel inquired.

"Awful," Sam said. "Well, except for Andrew's parents and Elizabeth, I guess." He sighed and headed into the family room.

"Those friends thou hast, and their adoption tried, grapple them unto thy soul with hoops of steel," came a familiar high-pitched voice from within the Mount Vernon bag, which was lying near the sofa. Sam jumped. The hat? Was it awake again?

"What?" Sam said, confused.

"Shakespeare," the hat said. "Hamlet." And it gave a sniff.

"I think the idea is to hold on to old friends," Nigel said hesitantly. "But I haven't taken a Shakespeare course in a while."

"I tried to hold onto him!" Sam said indignantly. "But Andrew's been taken over by Ryan, and by Tom, and by all this travel team stuff!"

"What is the meaning of this 'travel team'?" the hat inquired. "Where dost it travel?"

"It's a baseball team," Sam explained. "Of kids who are really good at baseball. And my best friend, or my old best friend who isn't really my friend any more, well, he's on one of those teams now. You know, they travel around the area and play other kids who are really good."

"Hmmm." The hat seemed to take this information in. "Base ball again," it said. "Please take me out of this bag."

Sam did.

"Well, I may not know much about base ball, but if there's something I do know about, it's travel," the hat said, seeming to puff out its chest. "So we'll show them, won't we! Now, where should we travel? Valley Forge? Philadelphia? Mount Vernon again?"

Just then, the doorbell rang, causing the hat to quiver. "Upon my soul," it shrieked. "What is that infernal noise?" The doorbell kept ringing and ringing, and Sam ran over to the front door. "Who is it?" he called, having been trained never to open the door to unfamiliar people.

"It's J. P.," came an excited voice from outside. "Do you want to see my new Lego that I just built?" Sam pulled the door open to find Ava's stepbrother, proudly holding up a complicated Lego vehicle. It must be the one Ava was complaining about the other day, Sam figured.

"Sure, come in," Sam said.

"Hey, Nigel," J. P. said, heading for the family room. "Look! I built it all by myself in the past four and a half hours!"

"Cool," Nigel said, examining the vehicle.

"It has three separate engines and four wings," J. P. continued. "Ava wouldn't help me build it, but I managed to do the whole thing without her."

"What on earth is the child babbling about?" the hat inquired.

"Who was that?" J. P. asked, startled.

Oh, boy, Sam thought. How can I explain the hat?

"It was I," the hat said.

"Oh," J. P. said, turning to Sam. "How'd you make it talk? Are you taking a ventriloquism class or something?"

"Ventriloquism," the hat said, sniffing again. "Certainly not. Sam does not cause me to talk. I speak for myself."

Sam held his breath. If J. P. found out about the hat, he'd probably tell Ava, who would tell Samantha, and soon the whole fifth grade would know. And the hat was his own private discovery.

"Wow!" J. P. said, accepting the idea of a talking hat fairly easily, Sam thought.

"This is a secret," Sam said sternly. "Only Nigel and I, and now you, know about this hat. Okay? No telling anyone, especially Ava."

"No way will I tell Ava," J. P. said. "Or anyone else, either. Wow! This is so phenomenal!"

"And where do you come from?" the hat inquired of J. P.

"Oh, across the street," J. P. replied, waving his hand toward his house. "I mean, when I'm with my dad. Sometimes I'm with my mom. And sometimes I visit my grandparents in France."

"So you are French!" the hat said warmly. "Do you know my friend the Marquis de Lafayette? Very helpful people, the French. Except when they weren't so helpful. But that was much earlier."

It paused, as if thinking. Sam, Nigel, and J. P. looked at one another and then back at the hat, wondering if it would continue, and if so, what it would say.

"Aha!" the hat said suddenly, startling the three of them. "We shall visit that earlier time!"

"What earlier time?" Sam asked, somewhat bewildered by what the hat had been saying. J. P. and Nigel nodded.

"The French and Indian Wars!" the hat exclaimed, sounding very pleased with itself. "General Washington, of course then he was only a colonel, was leading a group of colonials, helping the British fight the French."

"That's right," Nigel said, nodding. "This was back in the 1750s."

"The general had his ups and downs, I must say," the hat said, seeming to be lost in a reverie of some sort. "Some dangerous times during that period. But he did learn quite a lot."

"So?" J. P. burst in. "When can we go there? How will you get us there?"

"Us?" The hat turned toward J. P. "The rules of this magic call for Sam to travel, not the rest of you."

"Oh, come on, please?" J. P. begged. "It would be so fun!"

"I'd rather like to come along, too," Nigel said.

"No, you're far too big," the hat said decisively, turning toward Nigel. "I don't think it would work to bring you along. But you . . ." it turned back to J. P. "You might be able to hang onto me and I could eke out just enough strength to drag you along, too."

"Yes!" J. P. exulted, giving Sam a high-five.

Nigel looked disappointed. "Well, maybe another time," he said, and headed off to the basement.

Sam grabbed the hat, not wanting to waste another moment. "Okay, hold on!" he ordered J. P., who clasped both hands around the hat's brim as Sam put it on.

Sam prepared himself for the dizzy feeling, but this time it didn't come. Maybe he was getting used to the time-travel experience. Instead, he heard shrieks coming from J. P., and suddenly he saw the colors of the room start to whirl together, and then J. P.'s shouts were mingling with more shouts, those of hundreds of men, and the frantic neighing of horses, and when things settled down, he found himself with the hat on his head and a nervous-looking J. P. next to him in the middle of what looked like a forest.

"Help!" J. P. yelled. "Where are we?"

"Calm down!" Sam said, although he felt kind of nervous too. "Let's try to figure it out before you get us into trouble!"

Three men, dressed in red uniforms, sweat pouring down their faces, dashed past. "It's General Braddock," one of them was saying. "He's very badly hurt. We need to find Colonel Washington immediately!"

Sam perked up his ears. So George must be somewhere around. This must be a battle in the midst of the French and Indian Wars. He didn't expect much help from the hat in terms of untangling the history; as he remembered, the hat didn't say anything during these adventures.

Another red-uniformed man on a horse rode past, seemingly in a huge hurry. The sounds of the horse's hooves faded away.

"So where are we?" J. P. asked again. "Where's the actual battle? I think we should find it!"

Sam wasn't so sure. Actual battles had actual guns, and swords, and while that was all very well in a play or book, he wasn't eager to experience it in person. But J. P. was darting ahead through the forest and he had to keep an eye on him, didn't he? So he plunged through the underbrush after J. P.

Suddenly something whizzed past Sam's head and he instinctively ducked down and covered his head. He sensed a gasp from the hat. "Look out, J. P.!" Sam cried. "I think we're really close to the battle!"

"Hey, cool!" J. P. said, not ducking down at all, his earlier nervousness apparently a thing of the past. "Come on, let's go this way!"

Sam couldn't decide whether J. P. was brave or just too young to know any better. Just then, a couple more soldiers, also on horseback, appeared through the trees. Their red coats were starkly visible against the browns and greens of the forest. "Boys," one of them hailed them, "has either of you seen Colonel Washington? General Braddock has been wounded, and we need the colonel to take command."

"No, but we can help you look," Sam said. "Come on, J. P."

The two soldiers helped Sam and J. P. onto their respective horses, and they galloped off through the woods. As they proceeded, Sam could hear more shouts, cries, and hoofbeats. Were they getting closer to the actual battle? Something whizzed past their heads again, and the soldiers kicked at their horses to go faster.

They came to the crest of a hill, and as they headed downward, Sam could see a terrible scene unfolding as soldiers clashed with one another. Bayonets battled bayonets. Gunshots rang out. Soldiers fell off their horses, only to lie motionless on the ground. Riderless horses ran about, neighing in a frenzy. The sun glinted through the trees, a hot summer-type of sun. Sam wondered what month he was in. It felt a lot hotter than the late September weather he had left at home.

Suddenly Sam spied a tall, familiar figure on horseback in the midst of the battle. He was fending off one attacker from behind, and when he had finished with him, he dealt with another one approaching from the side.

"Colonel Washington!" the soldier on Sam's horse yelled above the sounds of battle. George turned around, wheeling his horse in the direction of Sam, J. P., and the two soldiers. "Colonel Washington, sir! General Braddock's been badly wounded and we need you to take command!"

"Where is the general?" George inquired, spurring the horse closer toward them.

"He's been taken back behind the lines, sir, but the lines really aren't what they were, with so many of our side lost, and . . ." the soldier trailed off.

"Yes, I see," George said. "Show me the right direction, and we'll all head over together."

"Yes, sir," the two soldiers said together, and they all

started off through the woods, chaos around them. At one point, the soldier on the horse with J. P. locked bayonets with an enemy soldier who had crept up from behind a bush, but J. P.'s soldier was able to get away without being hurt. J. P. shrieked and then hit his soldier on the back in a congratulatory manner. "Wow!" he cried. "That was incredible!"

"Thank you, I'm sure," the soldier said, looking at J. P. in a somewhat puzzled fashion as the horses sped onward. "We're getting closer now, sir," the soldier told George, who nodded. Then George seemed to take notice of the two boys.

"And how did you two end up in the fighting?" he inquired, looking over at Sam and J. P. during what seemed to be a moment of relative calm in the combat. "Wait, you look familiar," he said to Sam, his eyes narrowing in concentration. "I've seen you somewhere before!"

"Yes, I'm Sam," Sam explained quickly. "I met you a long time ago, when you were considering joining the navy."

"Of course!" George said, smacking his head with his hand. "And you were so very helpful, too. Very wise. I always wondered what had become of you! One minute you were there, and the next, poof!"

Sam wasn't sure what to say, but suddenly they heard a fusillade of gunshots nearby, and then another enemy soldier was right in front of them, and George saw to him with a whack of his sword. Sam wondered if George would be puzzled, given that while George was about a decade older than he had been when they first met, Sam was still a ten-year-old. But maybe the magic had taken care of that, because George didn't seem to notice anything out of the ordinary.

"Two horses shot out from under me during this dreadful battle, Sam," George said as the five of them continued riding. "And so many of my men lost. A sad business."

"Yes," Sam said, nodding sympathetically. He was feeling incredibly hot and sweaty, as well as somewhat terrified. His T-shirt was soaked through with sweat, as, he noticed, was J. P.'s.

J. P. leaned over from his nearby horse. "Hey," he called over to Sam. "What about me? Can't you introduce me?"

"Oh, sorry," Sam said. "George, I mean, Colonel, this is my friend J. P., from back home."

They had come into a quieter area of the forest, away from the fighting. "Very nice to make your acquaintance," George said, nodding at J. P. "Any friend of Sam's is a friend of mine."

"Hey, George," J. P. said, assuming instant familiarity. "Do you want to see a Lego I just built? Not the big one, but this is a smaller one I just put in my pocket before I went over to Sam's house. It's a Star Wars™ ship."

The two soldiers and George appeared to be intrigued, watching intently as J. P. pulled out a small gray and black Lego model from his pocket and held it out to George, who carefully took it as the horses slowed down.

Sam rolled his eyes. Showing Legos to George Washington seemed a little crazy to him, but George was turning the Lego over in his hands and studying it intently.

"Star Wars, you said?" George inquired curiously, looking over at J. P. "A ship that fights in the stars?"

"Well, it's from the movie," J. P. burbled on, seeming not to know or care that George and his fellow eighteenth-century soldiers would have no clue what he was talking about. "You know, with Luke Skywalker and Darth Vader."

George turned to Sam as if for a translation. "It's something that's very popular in Bethesda. In Maryland. Where we come from," Sam said.

"No, that's not true," J. P. promptly contradicted him, as the horses began moving again. "*Star Wars* is popular all over the world! And it has been for decades and decades!"

Sam sighed. "Yes, but not in 1750-whatever, where we are right now!" he hissed warningly at J. P.

"Oh, right," J. P. said. "I forgot."

The riders were pulling up to a clearing and Sam could see a man lying on the ground in apparent pain, with several other soldiers gathered around him.

"General Braddock," George cried, leaping off his horse. The other two horses also came to a halt and the soldiers jumped down, leaving Sam and J. P. to jump off awkwardly.

"Oh, Colonel Washington," the general said weakly. "My time has come. I need you to get word to the outside of what has happened here."

"General, you will still rally," George said encouragingly. "But of course, sir, I will get the word out, and will wind things up the best way I can."

"We have suffered terrible losses here," the general continued, barely able to get the words out. The others leaned in to hear him. "We must . . ." but his words trailed off and he lay back again.

"Please summon the doctor," George said urgently, turning to the two soldiers. "Sam and J. P., you come with me." And George leaped back onto his horse, pulling the two boys up in front of him.

"Where are we going?" Sam asked breathlessly as the horse plunged forward, picking up speed. "Are we going to meet with the French generals now? Maybe try to wind things up?" Before George could answer, a thought struck Sam. "You know, J. P. could help translate. He speaks French."

"That's right, George!" J. P. cried excitedly, his voice coming out unevenly as they bounced up and down on the horse. "I'm bilingual!"

"That certainly could be useful, yes," George said thoughtfully. "We'll need some help with the negotiations."

The horse, which was galloping quickly, suddenly reared into the air and leaped over a short bush in its way. As it did, Sam felt the hat come off his head. In a

panic, he managed to grab it before it flew away, but the next thing he knew, he and J. P. were sitting back in Sam's family room. A key was turning in the front door. Sam's parents.

"Hi, sweetie, hi, J. P.," Sam's mother said, smiling obliviously, giving Sam a hug and waving at J. P. "How nice that you could come over!"

Sam's dad grinned at them both. "Having fun, boys?"

J. P. recovered before Sam. "Absolutely! You wouldn't believe how much fun we've been having! I was about to pull off some major negotiations with the French! But then Sam's hat fell off, and we had to leave George back in the 1750s."

Sam's parents looked puzzled, and seemed on the verge of asking questions, so Sam gulped and jumped in. "Yeah, um, J. P.'s been showing me the Lego he made."

"Oh, dang, and George still has my Star Wars ship!" J. P. exclaimed.

"George from down the street?" Sam's mother asked, referring to a third-grader who lived a few houses away.

"Yeah," Sam said, giving J. P. a look.

"Right." J. P. nodded.

Sam, still holding his hat, sighed. George Washington was undoubtedly heading off for some important negotiations and now Sam wouldn't get to see what happened next. Beyond disappointed, he carefully put the hat back in its Mount Vernon bag. As he did, the hat seemed to wink at him.

Chapter ~4~

Oliver was standing on the stage in the all-purpose room, waving around a large foam sword. "Take that, you dastardly Tory," he cried. On his head was a white wig and a hat similar to Sam's special hat, and he was wearing a blue jacket with gold trim.

Ryan, who was playing a red-coated British soldier, collapsed at Oliver's feet as some of the other kids laughed.

It was Monday morning and the class was performing a dress rehearsal of their George Washington play, which was to be unveiled to the public in a few days. Sunday had passed quietly for the hat, and thus for Sam, who had kept busy with a variety of non-magic activities while stealing glances at the hat from time to time. But it remained quiet in its Mount Vernon bag.

As Oliver waved the sword through the air and continued declaiming various phrases, Sam frowned. Something just didn't look right. That wasn't the way George handled his sword. Sam, who was in costume as a colonial soldier, was supposed to be offstage at that point, but he couldn't help himself.

"Hey, Oliver," Sam called, edging onto the stage. "I think you should be holding the sword a little higher, see?" He moved over and adjusted the sword, nodding. That seemed better. More like how George would have done it.

"How do you know?" Oliver asked, somewhat rudely. "I think the way I was holding it was fine. And you're interrupting one of my speeches!"

"Yes, Sam, it's not your turn to be on stage right now," Ms. Martin chimed in. "You're in the next scene."

"But that's not the way George Washington held his sword," Sam said stubbornly. "I mean, when he was fighting the French, back in the 1750s, he kind of did this," and Sam demonstrated what he remembered George doing. Quick, that's how George moved. Demolishing the enemy.

"Come on, Sam, this isn't your part," Ava said. "And Oliver's right—how do you know how George Washington held his sword and moved around, anyway?"

"Yeah," added Samantha, her faithful sidekick.

"But . . ." Sam said. But what could he say? Ava apparently was completely in the dark about Sam's personal acquaintance with George; J. P. had kept his word. "Well, okay, I was just trying to help."

Oliver really wasn't doing such a great job as George, anyway, Sam muttered to himself as he waited for his turn on the stage. He could have done much better.

His annoyance continued throughout the school day, and was compounded by the fact that Oliver decided to walk home with Sam from the afternoon bus stop, not seeming to notice that Sam wasn't being especially nice or communicative. But then Oliver never seemed to notice things like that, Sam reflected as they arrived at Sam's front walkway.

"Well, gotta go now," Sam said, gesturing toward his house. Oliver, however, didn't take the hint.

"You want to play some chess?" Oliver asked.

"Like, now?" Sam asked. "Um . . ." He tried to come up with a plausible excuse as he moved closer to his front door, but Oliver came right along with him.

"I know I can beat you," Oliver said. "I mean, I didn't beat you at chess club last spring, but I think I've improved over the past few months." Chess club was resuming later that week after a summer hiatus, and Sam was looking forward to it. Oh, well, maybe a game of chess wouldn't hurt. He hadn't been playing a lot lately.

"Okay, sure, come on," he said, as Oliver followed him into the house.

Nigel appeared in the front entryway, raising one eyebrow—a trick Sam wished he could do—and shooting Sam a look of surprise as Oliver followed Sam into the house. Nigel was aware of how annoying Sam found Oliver.

"We're going to play a little chess and then I have lots of homework to do," Sam said. Not that Oliver would take the hint—he probably would just sit down and do homework right along with Sam.

They pulled the chess set out, and Sam soon was lost in figuring out various moves. Oliver did seem to have improved over the summer, with his chess if not his personality.

Nigel sat reading a thick book, some history text, probably, in the adjoining kitchen. All was quiet.

Just then, a loud yawn sounded from the Mount Vernon bag. "Is no one here?" the hat inquired, sounding annoyed. "Where is everyone?"

Oh, no, not again! Sam couldn't understand why the hat couldn't wait until just Sam was there, or just Sam and Nigel were there, to start talking. Oliver, however, who was bent over the chessboard and was breathing nasally, didn't seem to have heard anything, much to Sam's relief.

"I say, Sam, I'm feeling most confined in here!" the hat continued. "How about a little breath of fresh air?"

Oliver stirred. "Was that your cousin?" he said absent-mindedly, his eyes still on the chessboard and his hand on one of his pawns.

"Uh, yeah, that was Nigel. I guess he needs to take a walk or something," Sam said. "Hang on just a second." He jumped up, reached for the Mount Vernon bag, and carried it quickly up to his room, where he opened the windows, took the hat out of the bag, and laid the hat carefully on his bed.

"Okay, now you can have some nice fresh air," Sam told the hat.

"Why, thank you kindly," the hat said, yawning again, burping, and seeming to stretch. "Pardon me."

"I'll be back up in a little while," Sam said, running back down to the family room, where Oliver didn't seem to have moved or to have noticed that Sam was gone.

"Hey, Oliver," Nigel called from the kitchen. Oliver didn't reply. "Oliver!" Nigel got up from the kitchen chair and headed over to where Oliver was sitting. "Do your parents, or your baby sitter or whoever, know that you're over here?"

"Huh?" Oliver said, still in a fog. "Oh. No, I didn't tell anyone."

"Well, maybe you should," Nigel said, handing Oliver his cell phone.

"Okay," Oliver said. "I'll call my sisters. They're in high school and they look after me in the afternoons." He dialed a number and a flow of words came pouring out the other end. Oliver listened. "Yeah, at Sam's. But . . ." He listened some more. "Okay," he said, and without saying goodbye or anything like that, he handed the phone back to Nigel. "Well, looks like I need to go home," he said. "I guess my sisters were kind of mad because I actually need to go to Tae Kwon Do in fifteen minutes and they didn't know where I was."

"Yeah, I suppose they would be kind of upset," Nigel said, nodding.

"Okay, well, bye, Oliver," Sam said, trying to steer Oliver toward the front door. Oliver seemed reluctant to leave and kept eyeing the chessboard.

"We can play again some other time," Sam said. "All right?"

"Yeah, okay," Oliver said, and he finally left.

"I'm glad he didn't hear the hat," Sam said to Nigel, and he rushed back up to his room to bring the hat downstairs.

"All this up and down, up and down," the hat grumbled. "I was feeling very peaceful in your chamber."

"How are you today?" Sam inquired. "Well rested?

Up for an adventure?"

"I do feel rather well rested," the hat said, sounding surprised. "Perhaps I am acclimating to this twenty-first century after all."

Nigel's cell phone rang and he picked it up. "Celia!" he exclaimed, and, cell phone in hand, hurried down the stairs to the basement.

"And who might Celia be?" the hat asked.

"Nigel's girlfriend," Sam said. "Or someone he hopes will be his girlfriend. I guess she isn't really yet."

"Ah, true romance." The hat sighed. "I was there, you know, when the general first met Mrs. Washington."

"Really?" Sam said, intrigued.

"Oh, yes," the hat said. "Shall we?"

"Sure," Sam replied, reaching out and putting the hat firmly onto his head. As the room began to fade away, he thought that maybe he should have told Nigel where he was going, but it was too late now. The colors were spinning around, forcing Sam to close his eyes, and then he heard the sound of voices and music.

Curious, he opened his eyes to find himself sitting on a soft, fabric-covered chair in what looked like a fancy, old-fashioned living room. The wooden floors were covered with floral rugs, and sunlight slanted through the long windows. There was no one else in the room, but the voices seemed to be coming from a nearby space. Sam sank back in the chair, a sense of peacefulness coming over him.

Just then, two small children, a boy and a girl, ran into the room. "Who are you?" the little boy asked. They were wearing eighteenth-century clothes, sort of ruffly and dressed-up. The girl, possibly his sister, looked too young to talk. She put a finger in her mouth and looked questioningly at Sam.

"I'm Sam," he said. "I'm, um, visiting here." Who were these children, he wondered. Were they the grandchildren whose statues were at Mount Vernon? But then there wouldn't be grandchildren at this point, right? The hat had said they were going back to the time when George met Martha. "Who are you?"

"Jacky Parke Custis," the boy said, sounding somewhat self-important. "And this is my sister, Patsy."

"Do you know George Washington?" Sam asked. Might as well find out if he was in the right place, after all.

"Oh, yes!" the boy said. "He's in the parlor, with Mamma and some of the other people. Come on!" And he took Sam's arm and pulled him forward, in the manner of Andrew's sister Elizabeth. Patsy toddled behind them.

The voices and music grew louder, and Sam entered another large room. A woman was playing a small piano-like instrument at one end, and about a dozen people were conversing in groups. Sam looked around for George and spotted him in the far corner seated next to a woman. She had a round, pleasant face, and the two of them seemed engrossed in conversation.

"Mamma! Mamma!" Jacky cried, making haste across the room toward the pleasant-faced woman. "Look who we found!"

"Why, it's Sam!" George exclaimed, a half-smile forming on his face. "Just when I had given up hope of seeing you again!"

"Yes, it's Sam!" Jacky exclaimed. "But why is he here? Can he roll hoops with me?"

"Sam, this is Mrs. Martha Parke Custis," George said. "We are to be married soon. Perhaps you will be able to attend the ceremony?"

"So very glad to make your acquaintance, Sam," Martha said, smiling kindly at Sam, George, and the children, who both climbed onto her lap.

"Oh, yes, and you, too," Sam said, feeling somewhat overwhelmed. "I mean, congratulations to you both, and if I can, I would really like to come to your wedding." He sent the hat a thought wave, asking if he could stick around long enough for the wedding, but didn't get any sense that the hat had picked up the vibration.

"And these are the children," George said, casting a fond eye upon them. "Jacky and Patsy. But I suppose you've already made their acquaintance."

"Yes," Sam said.

"I was about to take Sam and his friend to see the French commander," George explained to Martha. "This was during the fighting, you know. But all of a sudden they were gone! I hope you didn't run into any trouble." He turned to Sam.

"Oh, no, not at all," Sam said. He wasn't entirely sure how many years ago the last adventure had taken place and really wished the hat would speak up and tell him. But the hat remained quiet.

"Yes, we are to live at Mount Vernon after we are married," Martha said. "And the children are so happy to have a new papa."

That's right, Martha was a widow when George married her, and the children were from her first marriage, Sam remembered Ms. Martin telling them. George and Martha didn't have any more children together.

"Come on, Sam," Jacky said, hopping off Martha's lap. "I should like to play outside with you."

"Okay," Sam said. "If that's all right with your mom."

Martha nodded. "Very well. But Jacky, please do what Sam tells you."

"Hurrah!" Jacky cried, and pulled Sam out of the room into a sweep of green grass.

"I left my hoop out here," he said. "Let me call Josiah and ask him where it is." He let out a scream. "Josiah! Josiah! Where's my hoop?"

A boy about Sam's age hurried around the corner of the house. Unlike Jacky and Patsy, the boy was wearing very plain cotton clothes that looked mended and patched. He was African-American. Sam gulped. Was he a slave?

"Here, Master Jacky," Josiah said, handing the small boy a hoop. He looked curiously at Sam.

"Hi," Sam said. "My name's Sam, and I'm visiting. From Maryland."

"I'm Josiah," the boy said. "I live here."

"Josiah?" came a woman's voice. "Where did you go?"

"I must get back to the house," Josiah said, giving Sam another curious look.

"Well, nice to meet you," Sam said.

"Yes, same to you," Josiah said, and disappeared around the corner of the house.

"Well?" Jacky Parke Custis said impatiently, holding the hoop out to Sam. "Are we not going to play?"

Sam would much rather have talked some more with Josiah, but that didn't seem likely to happen, so he took the hoop. "Okay, sure," he said, trying to think of what to do with it. "Do we just roll it?" He pushed it along.

"Yes, of course we roll it!" Jacky exclaimed, grabbing the hoop back and propelling it by his side as he ran through the lawn. "You're awfully silly for such a big boy." He looked around, and picked up a large stick. "Here, you can push it along with the stick."

Sam took a turn, pushing the hoop with the stick as he ran next to Jacky, slowing down to accommodate the smaller boy's steps. Hey, this was kind of fun, he thought. Maybe he would get really good at hoop-rolling and could stay back here in the eighteenth century, and join the equivalent of the hoop-rolling travel team. Maybe . . .

His thoughts were interrupted by Jacky. "May I try on your hat?" Jacky inquired.

"Well, I'm sorry, but, no, you can't," Sam said. The hat needed to remain on his own head, or who knew what would happen.

"But I want to!" Jacky said. "Please?"

"No, I'm really sorry," Sam said. "It's kind of a special hat, and it has to stay on my head."

"I want to try your special hat!" Jacky said, his lip starting to quiver. "I want to!" And he started to cry.

Oh, no, Sam thought. Now he'd gone and upset George Washington's soon-to-be stepson. Martha wouldn't be happy either. But he couldn't let Jacky try on the hat, could he?

Sam's reverie was ended when Jacky suddenly stopped crying, and began to giggle. "I know what I shall do!" Jacky said excitedly. And before Sam could stop him, he reached out, plucked the hat from Sam's head, and started to put it on his own.

Sam reacted too slowly and reached for the hat, only to feel the familiar whirling feeling. It was accompanied this time by childish squeals and shrieks. He shuddered to think of what might be happening and hoped that the squeals and shrieks would remain back in the eighteenth century.

But no. Sam found himself back in his family room with his hat—and with Jacky Parke Custis!

"Where am I?" Jacky cried, looking around. "I want Mamma!" And he burst into tears again.

Nigel came running up the stairs from the basement.

"What is going on here?" he demanded. "Who is this? And where did you go without telling me?"

"Sorry, Nigel," Sam said. "I should have told you. But this is Jacky Parke Custis. George Washington's stepson."

Jacky Parke Custis continued to weep. "I want Mamma!" he bawled. "I want my new papa! I want Patsy!"

"Oh, what have you done now," Nigel said, taking a deep breath and looking at Sam. "This isn't good."

Suddenly the hat spoke. "I can remedy the situation," it said in its high-pitched voice. "But I need some time to rest and recuperate. I am just exhausted."

Jacky turned toward the hat, startled out of his crying. "A talking hat?" he said. "I want that!"

"No," Sam said. "That's what caused all this trouble in the first place. We need to figure out how to get you home!"

"I will take young Master Jacky home," the hat said. "But first I must take a nap." And a moment later it was snoring.

"Jacky, it's all right," Nigel said comfortingly. "We'll get you back home. Would you like something to eat?"

"No," Jacky said, wiping his eyes with his white shirt. "I want to play with the talking hat."

"Well, it's taking a little nap," Nigel said. Sam nodded. "What about this robot?" Nigel said, pulling an old toy of Sam's out of a basket. "It talks."

"Danger, danger, Will Robinson," the robot intoned.

Jacky picked up the robot, entranced. Sam hadn't played with it in a long time, but it used to be one of his favorites, a replica from the old TV show *Lost in Space*. He had the whole set of *Lost in Space* videos and had watched them over and over.

"Danger, danger, Will Robinson," Jacky said, seemingly over his tears. "This is great fun!"

"We need to figure something out before your parents get home," Nigel said to Sam. "I'm not sure how we could explain Jacky to them."

"You're right," Sam said. "Although they don't seem to notice anything out of the ordinary, do they?" Maybe people over a certain age just weren't aware of the magic. Nigel was twenty, so maybe anyone over, say, twenty-one?

Just then, as if on cue, the door opened and Sam's dad came in, dropping his keys into a bowl near the front door and heading for the family room. "Hi, Sam, Nigel. I decided to leave a little early today," he said. "And who's your young friend?" he inquired, looking at Jacky.

"Danger, danger, Will Robinson," Jacky said, intent on the robot and not paying much attention.

"He's a friend from nearby," Sam said. This was somewhat true. Virginia wasn't too far away, after all.

"Oh," his father said. His father was often lost in his own train of thought, Sam reflected. "Well, nice to meet you."

"Nice to meet you, too," Jacky said, focusing now on Sam's father. "I'm Jacky Parke Custis."

Sam's father frowned, as if the name sounded vaguely familiar. "Jacky? Jacky Parke Custis? Now where have I heard that name?"

Sam remained quiet, hoping that the hat wouldn't choose this particular moment to wake up. He exchanged a meaningful glance with Nigel, eyeing the hat. Nigel gave an imperceptible nod.

"Uncle Phil," Nigel said to Sam's father. "Would you mind showing me where the replacements are for that overhead light fixture down in the basement? It's flickering."

"Sure," Sam's dad said, and followed Nigel down the basement steps.

Sam, seizing the opportunity, picked up the hat. "Please, you're going to have to wake up now and take Jacky back home!"

The hat stirred and made some grumbling noises. "I need to rest," it said, curling itself into a ball.

"But my dad's here, and I think my mom will be back in a few minutes, and . . ."

"They won't notice a thing," the hat said. It paused. "But perhaps Mrs. Washington, or Mrs. Parke Custis as she was then, will be upset if Jacky isn't back, yes, yes." It uncurled itself. "Very well, perhaps you're right."

Sam put the hat on his head and took Jacky by the hand. Jacky was still holding the robot. The room swirled around, and suddenly Sam, Jacky, and the robot were back on the green lawn outside the house. The hoop lay abandoned beside them.

Jacky bolted into the parlor toward his mother and George. "Look what Sam gave me!" he exclaimed. "Sam took me to his house and gave me this talking toy!"

"Danger, danger, Will Robinson," the robot said.

Martha and George looked startled. "What will they come up with next!" Martha exclaimed. "Where did you find such a toy, Sam?"

"Oh, it was a present," Sam said. What would a talking robot do left behind in the eighteenth century? But it seemed clear that Jacky wasn't about to give it up. "And now I've sort of outgrown it, so it's fine if Jacky keeps it."

"Thank you, Sam," Martha said. "I know Jacky has quite a vivid imagination, so I suppose he thought he was at your house. You know how small children can be."

"Right," Sam said. "Vivid imagination, absolutely."

"How long will you be staying this time, Sam?" George inquired. "Will you be able to attend the wedding?"

"I'd like to," Sam said. "My plans are a little, um, uncertain." He sat down on a chair next to George. Patsy, who had been on Martha's lap, climbed down and immediately climbed onto Sam's lap. "Hat!" she said, reaching for Sam's hat.

The last thing Sam needed was baby Patsy coming back with him to Bethesda, so he reached for the hat to get it from Patsy's grasp. But as he did so, the room swirled around him, and he found himself a moment later back home in his family room.

No Jacky. No Patsy. That was good. But his mother stood there, a puzzled look on her face. "Sam?" she said. "One minute you weren't there, and then you just . . . appeared!"

"Oh, I was just outside and I ran back in," Sam said, improvising wildly. "You know, I'm a fast runner. I just sprinted right in!"

"Well, all right," his mom said, sounding doubtful, but reaching out to give Sam a big hug. "Did you have a good day, sweetheart?"

"Yes, I guess I did," Sam said. "Busy, but good."

"All ready for the George Washington play?" his mom asked. "I can't wait to see it!"

"Of course!" Sam said. "I mean, we have a couple more rehearsals, but it's coming along. I just wish I could have been George. I feel like I could have done a better job than Oliver."

"Sam, maybe Ms. Martin just wanted to give someone else a chance," his mom said soothingly.

"But I know George," Sam said. "I mean, I know how he would react, and how he moves around, and how . . ."

"You do have a vivid imagination," his mother said fondly. "You always have!"

Recess had always been one of Sam's favorite parts of the school day. He and Andrew had spent years exploring every part of the playground and adjoining field, or playing soccer or kickball with some of the other boys.

But this year, recess had become torture. Andrew was always with Ryan and Tom, who were, and always had been, the bosses of the group of boys who played soccer or kickball. Ryan and Tom determined whether it would be soccer or kickball that day, and even who would play on which team. Sam remembered one day, back in third grade, when he and Andrew had tried to get Ryan and Tom to change from soccer to kickball, because he and Andrew liked kickball better, but Ryan and Tom had said no, and had been pretty mean about it, too.

There were, of course, some boys who didn't join in the soccer or kickball game, who hung around on the playground equipment, or made up imaginary games, or, in a few cases, played with the girls. This year, Sam felt betwixt and between, sort of drifting around during recess. He didn't feel comfortable  trying to play kickball or soccer because things were too weird with Andrew. Sometimes he played with some of those other non-soccer-and-kickball-playing boys. Sometimes he talked to Oliver. Sometimes he even hung around with Ava and Samantha. Today, everyone seemed busy. Even Oliver was occupied, practicing a scene with Katie, the girl who played Martha Washington.

Sam moodily kicked a stone along one of the pathways that lined the school's play area. He looked over toward the group of boys who were, today, playing kickball. Andrew was up, and Sam watched as Tom expertly rolled the ball toward Andrew, Andrew bashed the ball over Tom's head, and Ryan, who was in left field, rushed in to catch it. "Good catch, Ryan!" a couple of kids called. Andrew joined the other kids waiting for their turn to kick. He seemed to look in Sam's direction, but Sam turned his head away.

Just then, the whistle blew for the end of recess, much to Sam's relief. But then came lunch, another former pleasure that had turned less than pleasant.

Today, he watched Andrew, Tom, and Ryan as they sat at one end of the table, joking around and laughing. He put his own lunchbox down next to Ava's and Samantha's.

"So what's up with J. P.?" Ava asked Sam as she bit into her tuna sandwich. "Remember when he went over to your house the other day?"

Sam nodded, his heart sinking. "Uh-huh." Had J. P. let something slip about their adventure?

"He just hasn't been acting the same since then. Nothing seems exciting enough for him! He won't play with his Legos or anything. He just keeps saying it's all really boring. I keep asking him what you guys did over there, but he won't tell me."

Well, at least he wasn't saying anything. That was good. "Hmmm." Sam said, stalling for time.

"He's probably just going through a phase," Samantha said, sounding like a junior psychiatrist. "You know, maybe he's just getting more grown-up or something."

"J. P.? More grown-up?" Ava snorted. "I don't think so. Oh, well. So my Boston trip is only a few days away now!"

"That's right!" Samantha said. Sam breathed a sigh of relief. A new topic!

"Why are you going to Boston?" he asked.

"Oh, my aunt's getting married. My mom and my aunt, both getting married in the same year! But my aunt doesn't have any kids, or stepkids either, for that matter."

Sam reflected on Ava's situation. Her dad lived in California, and every summer she went out there to spend the whole summer with him. She also went out there for winter vacation every year. And now she had this new stepdad and stepbrother, and even though Sam thought J. P. was a hilarious kid and would be kind of fun to have for a brother, maybe all these changes were hard for Ava. Maybe he should try to be more sympathetic, or empathetic, or whatever the right word was. His mom had reminded him of that a while back, but it hadn't really struck him in a serious way until now. He imagined some new person coming to live with his family. Well, Nigel had done just that, but Nigel was his cousin, and he already knew Nigel from various family visits over the years.

"Right, Sam?" Samantha was asking. He had spaced out again.

"Uh, yeah," Sam said, blinking. He had no idea what he was agreeing to, but agreement seemed like the right thing to do.

"You weren't listening to anything we said," Ava said accusingly.

"Sorry," Sam said, filled with a new resolution to try to get along better with Ava. Back when they were really little, when Ava and her mom had moved into the house across the street, he and Ava had been good friends. Or so his mom had told him. He couldn't really remember. "I was thinking about something else."

Ava launched into a long description of her various family members, and who was coming to the wedding, and what her aunt's dress looked like, and Samantha nodded and made approving comments, and Sam tried to do the same but found his mind wandering, and finally the bell rang and it was time to go back to the classroom.

Ms. Martin had written the word "slavery" on the board. An image of Josiah popped into Sam's head. He assumed Josiah was a slave. What would have happened if he had had more of a chance to talk to him? His mind flicked toward Andrew. Andrew's dad was African-American; his mom was white. If Andrew had been alive back then, living right there near what would become Washington, DC, would he, his dad, and Elizabeth all be slaves? It was too horrible to comprehend.

"In his will," Ms. Martin said, "George Washington freed all the slaves that belonged to him, but they were to be freed only after Martha's death."

Sam raised his hand, posing a question that he really wanted to ask George, not Ms. Martin. "How could George and the other founders of this country have had slaves, anyway, when they were writing things like the Declaration of Independence?"

"That's a really good question, Sam," Ms. Martin said. "It's hard to understand."

Other kids jumped into the discussion, and Sam found his thoughts returning again and again to Josiah. What was his life like? Had he been freed after George and Martha died? And how old would he have been by then, anyway? Probably around fifty-something years old, right?

"Sam?" Ms. Martin was asking.

"Oh, sorry," Sam said, feeling his face turning red.

"I was just thinking about this one particular boy, who I think was one of George's slaves. His name was Josiah, and he was around our age, I think." Sam gestured at his fellow classmates.

Ms. Martin looked puzzled. "Did you read about him, Sam?"

Sam stopped. Now why had he mentioned Josiah, anyway? He couldn't very well say that he had met him, could he? Ava and Samantha would burst their sides laughing at him. So would everyone else. "Yes, that's right," he said.

Ms. Martin nodded. "You really seem to have gone above and beyond with your research, Sam," she said. "That's the sign of a true scholar!" And she smiled at him.

Sam smiled back. Well, it was all thanks to the hat. But he couldn't tell Ms. Martin that, of course.

Ryan, who had been whispering to Tom through much of this exchange, started laughing really loudly.

"Ryan?" Mrs. Martin gave him a warning glance.

"Sorry," Ryan said, snorting and trying not to laugh.

Ms. Martin clapped her hands. "We're going to have one more rehearsal today, and we really need to be ready."

"Onward, as we cross the Delaware," Oliver pronounced, standing up next to his seat and assuming a stern look. Well, maybe Oliver was getting better at playing George, Sam thought grudgingly. He did seem to have captured something of George's facial expression. As the class headed off to the all-purpose room to rehearse, Sam caught up to Oliver. Might as well offer a compliment.

"I think you're doing well as George," Sam said. "Keep it up!"

Oliver looked surprised. "Thanks, Sam," he said, and a pleased look formed on his face. He hurried ahead of Sam to talk to Katie.

Sam thought of the hat. What would it think of their play? Maybe he should bring it in for the final performance and give it a chance to see the show. On the other hand, maybe it would create complete chaos. He would have to think about it. Or maybe ask the hat.

Once he got home, he did just that. The hat, which had been reclining in its Mount Vernon bag, jumped up and down with excitement. "Yes, yes indeed! I would very much like to see your performance!" it said in its high-pitched voice. "A play about General Washington, what could be finer! And with you playing a role! Very exciting!"

"I mean, usually I get a bigger part than I did this time," Sam said. "I'm just one of the soldiers. But maybe I could wear you! If you didn't send me back to the actual eighteenth century, that is."

"I promise," the hat squeaked. "I promise!"

The doorbell rang, and the hat shrieked. It still hadn't gotten used to the sound, Sam guessed.

"Oh," said Nigel, who had been sitting on the sofa. "It's Celia!" And he rushed to the door. "We're going to study for an exam."

Sam, holding the Mount Vernon bag with the hat, followed behind, curious to meet Celia.

Nigel opened the door. "Celia!" he said. "So great to see you! Come in!"

Celia, who was small and had a round face and curly hair, gave Nigel a quick hug and walked in. She sort of looked like a modern-day Martha Washington, Sam thought.

"Let me take your backpack," Nigel said. "And this is my cousin Sam."

As Sam and Celia said hello to each other, the hat decided to join in. "Ah, Celia!" it suddenly announced loudly from the Mount Vernon bag. "The girlfriend-to-be!"

Celia looked startled. "What was that?" she asked, looking around for an explanation.

Nigel turned toward Sam with a furious expression, indicating, without saying anything, that he, and especially the hat, should make themselves scarce.

"Okay," Sam said, grabbing the bag and starting up the stairs. "Sorry, Celia, it's this old toy of mine that I keep meaning to give away. It was just saying something, but I couldn't quite hear it."

"How rude, Sam!" the hat continued. "I was just attempting to participate." Sam, on the receiving end of another glare from Nigel, ran the rest of the way up the stairs and into his room, the hat protesting all the way. "A talking toy!" it said indignantly. "Something to give away? Well, really!"

"Sorry about that," Sam said. "But you shouldn't have said that about the girlfriend and all. It was kind of embarrassing for Nigel. I mean, maybe Celia doesn't even know he likes her!"

"Ah, yes," the hat said musingly. "The misunderstandings of courtship. Well, you did get to see Colonel and Mrs. Washington during their courtship, which went quite smoothly, I must say."

"Are we doing anything today?" Sam inquired. "Or are you too tired?"

"I am feeling sprightly and filled with energy!" the hat announced, to Sam's surprise. "Perhaps the twenty-first century is starting to agree with me, after all!"

"Well, so, where are we going?" Sam asked.

"I should think Valley Forge would provide a useful lesson," the hat said musingly. "You will remember what happened there?" And the hat seemed to look at Sam in a challenging sort of way.

Sam tried to remember what Ms. Martin had told the class about Valley Forge. "It was really cold there, right?" he said.

"Bitter cold," the hat said, shivering a little. "I remember the wind would blast through the walls of those log cabins the general had the soldiers build."

"And this was during the first couple of years of the war, right?" Sam asked, hoping to get his time frame right for the journey.

"We first arrived there in December 1777," the hat said, "after the British took Philadelphia. Valley Forge was not too far distant, and it seemed a good place for our encampment. But it was winter, and the snow was piled high." It paused, apparently reflecting on times past, before giving another little shiver. "Are you ready?"

Sam picked up the hat and put it on his head. As

the room dimmed around him, he realized that he was wearing a T-shirt and shorts, and that maybe he should have looked for his winter jacket and snow boots, but then he heard a howling sound, like a strong wind, all around him, and the sound of voices, and he found himself standing in a snowdrift in front of a half-built log cabin. But for some reason he didn't feel especially cold.

The young soldier hammering nails into the frame of the cabin did not seem to notice that Sam was wearing skimpy, twenty-first-century clothes unsuited to either the temperature or the time period.

"Hi, boy, ye here to help out?" the young man asked, tossing Sam an extra hammer.

"Uh, sure," Sam said. "What exactly are we doing?"

"Well, the general has ordered that we build these log cabins to sleep in," the soldier said. "Henry," he added, extending his hand. "From Boston."

Sam shook Henry's hand, then picked up the hammer and tried to follow what Henry was doing. "Sam," he said. "From Maryland." No point in saying that he was from near Washington, DC, because it hadn't been invented yet.

Henry stamped his feet, trying to stay warm. Sam noticed that Henry's clothes were worn and frayed and his shoes had several holes. "Blasted cold," Henry said. "Nothing to do but keep moving, keep working on these cabins. We're likely to be here a good many months."

"When did you arrive?" Sam inquired. He looked around. Rows of half-built cabins filled the field as far as Sam could see, and countless ragged-looking men were hard at work constructing their winter quarters.

"Oh, it's been a fortnight or so," Henry said. "First order of business is to build our quarters, and soon we will start training."

"For what?" Sam asked.

"Military discipline," Henry said, picking up his hammer again and landing some blows. "Those British beat us pretty bad, but we shall show them!"

"Yes, in the end, you shall," Sam said encouragingly.

"That's the spirit, boy!" Henry cried, clapping Sam on the back with his free hand.

"So where is the general?" Sam asked, curious to find George and see if he'd remember him. After all, the last time they had met was a couple of decades earlier, and perhaps George had other things on his mind.

"General Washington is in his quarters," Henry said, pointing across the field. "Are you off to explore?"

"Well, yes," Sam said, and then felt a little guilty. "Unless you'd like me to stay and help you, of course."

"No, no, go and look around," Henry said jovially. "It's been a pleasure to meet you."

"Yes, me too," Sam said. "I mean, you, too." And he headed off through the snow in the direction Henry had indicated. His sneakers, for some reason, didn't get wet, thanks to the hat and its magic, Sam supposed. And while he was starting to feel a little chilly, he didn't feel as cold as one might in the middle of winter wearing only a T-shirt and shorts.

Sam made his way past various men, all working on their houses. The wind was picking up, and he shivered. Many of the men, he noticed, were coughing. One bearded young man was bent over, deep racking coughs shaking his entire body. Hadn't Ms. Martin told the class that many of George Washington's men had died during that winter at Valley Forge?

Far in the distance, Sam spotted a stone house, and he thought that might be where George had set up his headquarters. As he made his way closer, he noticed some kids his own age, apparently helping their mothers with some washing. One boy was folding several worn-out-looking blankets.

"Excuse me," Sam said. "Is that General Washington's headquarters?"

"Yes, it is," the boy said. "I believe he's there right now, along with some of the other generals."

"Thanks," Sam said. He trudged through the banks of snow, which seemed to be increasing in size. Or maybe he was just getting colder and more tired.

Finally, the house was in front of him. The door was slightly open, and Sam pushed it open further. Inside he saw George, much older-looking now, with lines etched into his face that certainly hadn't been there the last time.

The general, dressed in a well-worn uniform with the jacket partly unbuttoned, sat around a table near a roaring fire with several other similarly attired men.

"The Congress simply must act," George was saying, pounding his hand on the table. "These men need provisions! They need shoes! Their clothes are ragged. And when is our German friend to arrive?"

Sam stepped a little closer and the floorboards creaked, causing George and his companions to turn around.

George, who had been frowning, peered at Sam, and slowly a pleased expression crossed his face. "Sam?" he said. "Is it really you? It's been so long!"

"Yes, sir, it is," Sam said, once more amazed that George remembered him and seemed unfazed by the fact that Sam never seemed to age.

"Gentlemen, my friend Sam," George said, beckoning Sam over to the table. The other generals, puzzled looks on their faces, murmured their greetings.

"A pleasure to meet you all," Sam said. He'd have to ask the hat later exactly who all these men were, but he assumed they were pretty high up in the Continental Army.

"I was just saying," George said to Sam, "that we're having some trouble with Congress."

"Yes, presidents often have trouble with Congress," Sam said without thinking. "Or at least that's what my parents are always talking about." Then he clapped his hand over his mouth. Of course, George wasn't the president yet. He probably didn't have any idea about being the president yet.

"President?" George said, frowning. "But we have no president."

"No, of course you don't," Sam said, shaking his head.

"Well," George said, "in any case, we need more money, and Congress has been very reluctant to provide it. It grows tiresome, Sam." He turned to the other generals. "I think our meeting has come to an end, gentlemen," he said, and the others, mumbling their farewells, shifted their chairs back from the table and made their way out of the room.

George leaned back in his chair, his hand resting contemplatively on his chin. "So what do you make of the situation, Sam?" he asked, his eyes boring into Sam's. "There are times, I confess, when I grow weary and discouraged. The men are brave, but they lack training. They lack food and warm clothing, and many of them are sick, even dying."

Sam nodded. The image of the teenaged George, upset at not getting to go to sea, popped into his head, and he realized that once again, he needed to encourage George.

"It will all work out," Sam said. "I know it seems difficult now, but things will turn around. You will triumph in the end, and the British will be defeated."

"Brave words, Sam," George said. "I hope you are correct." But he looked a little more encouraged, Sam thought. "Yes, we soon will have a German officer, Baron von Steuben, coming here to train the men," George continued. "Recommended by Benjamin Franklin, so I'm sure this fellow will be useful."

"When is he arriving?" Sam asked, curious. This could be interesting. Maybe he could learn some military trade craft just in time to incorporate into the school play. After all, he was playing a Revolutionary soldier.

"The Baron is making his way here, but it could be a month or more before his arrival," George said. "Mrs. Washington might well be here before the Baron."

"Oh, is Mrs. Washington going to be spending the winter here?" Sam vaguely remembered Samantha discussing this in her presentation to the class about Martha Washington, but he couldn't recall the details.

"Yes, and it will do my heart good to see her!" George exclaimed, stretching his feet toward the fire. Sam did the same. The fire felt really good, so nice and warm after the chill of the outdoors. Sam found that he was drowsy. He tilted his head back and, trying to cover his mouth so as not to be rude to George, yawned. As he did, the hat almost slipped off his head, but Sam managed to yank it back on before it came off completely and sent him back to the twenty-first century.

But the hat apparently had come off enough that Sam was no longer seated by the fire. Instead, he was back outside, standing in the snow, watching a column of men drilling on the white, chilly field. A man dressed in military regalia was standing in front of them, berating them in a foreign language. Sam had no idea what he was saying, but he sounded angry. The troops, though, seemed to respond well, their feet and their muskets moving in formation. Their uniforms, if you could call them that, were still ragged.

Sam looked around. George was nowhere to be seen. In the distance was his stone headquarters. Nearby were seemingly hundreds of log cabins. What was going on? What had happened? He was still at Valley Forge, that was clear, but was it still December of 1777?

A weary-looking soldier passed by, and Sam asked him the date.

"I couldn't tell you for certain, boy, but I'd say we're in February by now," the man responded.

"1778?" Sam asked.

"Why, yes, boy, 1778," the man said, shooting Sam a strange look before disappearing into one of the log cabins.

February 1778? So it was two months later. Had the lifting of the hat sent time into fast-forward? Like pushing a fast-forward button? The hat hadn't lifted off Sam's head enough to send him back home, but it had shifted the time nonetheless. A useful fact, Sam thought. Maybe he could play around with time on his next adventure. Lift the hat a little and advance a week. Lift it a little more and advance further. And what about backwards? The possibilities seemed endless.

Then a familiar figure came into sight as Sam recognized Henry, the first soldier he had met. "Henry from Boston!" Sam cried, glad to see someone he knew, if only slightly. "I'm Sam from Maryland, remember me?" He realized that for Henry, a couple of months had passed, so he wouldn't be surprised if Henry didn't remember him at all, but he did.

"Oh, yes, Sam from Maryland!" Henry said. "Haven't run into you for a while." He waved at the men who were drilling. "What do you think of all this?" he asked. "Just a few hand-picked men, and the Baron is training them. Then they will train all the rest of us."

Sam nodded. "The Baron looks kind of upset," he ventured.

Henry laughed. "Oh, yes, that's his way," he said. "So much cursing and swearing, but it's all in German, so I don't understand it at all. And then one of the officers translates it into French, but I don't understand that either." He chuckled. "But he seems to be getting his point across, whatever language he uses."

He did, Sam reflected. The men seemed to be following

along, executing their maneuvers with a truly military precision. Sam tried to capture it in his memory to use for the school play.

"Well, Sam, I'm off to try to find some food," Henry announced. "There never seems to be enough, so I'll have to try to forage." He clapped Sam on the shoulder and headed off.

Just then, a group of women and children hastened past Sam, and he noticed that Martha Washington was among them. Like George, she had aged, but her face still looked round and her eyes were twinkling. Several of the women were holding piles of clothing and blankets, and one of the boys was dispatched to bring the piles to the various cabins. The women stopped to watch the Baron and his pupils, and Sam decided to reintroduce himself to Martha.

He approached her, and she smiled. "You do look familiar, young man," she said.

"Yes," Sam said. "My name's Sam. I met you back in Virginia." He figured it didn't make sense to say that it was twenty years earlier, given that Sam certainly didn't look like he could possibly have been alive twenty years earlier.

"Why, yes!" Martha said, smiling warmly at Sam. "You're the kind young man who gave Jacky that wonderful toy! He played with it for years and years. Of course, Jacky's all grown up these days."

"That's right," Sam said. "Of course. I'm so glad he liked it!" Like George, Martha didn't seem to see the disconnect between the passage of time and the fact that Sam was still a boy. But maybe he looked like an adult. Could that be true? If so, how exciting! Was there a mirror around? He would have to consult with the hat. In his excitement, he pulled the hat off his head and couldn't react in time to stop himself. The wind whistled around his ears and suddenly he was in his room, at home in the twenty-first century again.

"But . . ." Sam said, reaching his hands out as if he could maybe figure out a way to get back to Valley Forge.

"I did my best that one time," the hat chirped; it had made its way back into the Mount Vernon bag. "I had to do some fancy thinking to keep you at Valley Forge, I did. Two months ahead, but still there. But this time you whipped me off your head so quickly, there was absolutely nothing I could do."

Sam nodded, acknowledging that the hat was probably right. "So tell me," he asked the hat. "Do I look older when I go back there? I mean, how come George and Martha never notice that I look like a kid, and they get older and older?"

"Magic works in funny ways," the hat said reprovingly. "I wouldn't begin to interfere if I were you!"

"I'm not trying to interfere," Sam protested. "I'm just curious."

"Curiosity killed the cat," the hat retorted. "A useful saying." And with that, it settled into its bag and began to snore.

Chapter ~6~

Much of Wednesday was taken up with rehearsals for the play, which was to be performed the next day. Sam managed to incorporate some of the Baron's teachings into his own role as a soldier, but ran into some trouble when he tried to get the other kids playing soldiers to join in and change the way they were standing and marching. They refused, as did Ms. Martin when he asked her if it might be possible for him to play the Baron instead of an ordinary soldier.

But that was okay, because after school was the first meeting of the chess club, something Sam was looking forward to. At dismissal time, he grabbed his backpack and hurried to the classroom down the hall where the chess club was meeting. Oliver hurried behind him. They made their way into the room, and Sam was glad to see Mr. Alexander, the chess teacher, waiting for them. Mr. Alexander, the grandfather of a boy who used to go to Eastview, was retired from his job and had been teaching chess for years.

As the kids gathered and Mr. Alexander began greeting everyone, Sam was surprised to see Ryan edge into the room and look around. Spotting Sam, he slid into the seat next to him, dropping his backpack onto the floor. What was Ryan doing here? He had never been in the chess club before. In fact, he had been known to make fun of the kids who were in the chess club. This was weird.

"Glad to see a new face," Mr. Alexander said, looking at Ryan. "What's your name?"

"Ryan," Ryan muttered.

"Excellent. Good to have you here," Mr. Alexander said. "Not that I'm not thrilled to have all my old regulars back again." He smiled at Sam and the other dozen kids, all of whom had been there before. "So have you played chess before, Ryan?"

Ryan shook his head. "Not really."

"Okay, what I'm going to do is pair you up with Sam, just for today," Mr. Alexander said. "He's been doing this for a long time, so he can show you some tricks of the trade." And he winked.

Sam wasn't sure how he felt about this. He had assumed he'd end up with Ben, a fourth-grader who was pretty good at chess and who had been his regular partner the previous year. Ben was also a lot nicer than Ryan. But Mr. Alexander was moving on, assigning Ben to play with Oliver.

"So, Sam, what can you show me?" Ryan said as Sam began to set up the chessboard. "I guess this is something you're actually good at, right?"

Sam sighed. As opposed to baseball, he supposed

Ryan meant. He began explaining the various pieces and how they could move around the board, and then he stopped, noticing a bored look on Ryan's face. "What are you doing here, anyway?" he asked Ryan. "I mean, I'm kind of surprised to see you."

"Learning to play chess, Sam, okay? Why are we all here?" Ryan said, gesturing around the room and sneering slightly.

Fair enough. But it did seem strange. Nevertheless, he continued his explanation. As he finished describing all the moves the queen could make, a flicker of interest seemed to appear in Ryan's eyes, and then Ryan slammed both hands down on the desk, causing the chess pieces to shift around.

"So let's play already," he exclaimed. "Enough of all these explanations."

"But . . ." Sam said. "I haven't described the rooks, or the knights, or . . ."

"Oh, forget about all that," Ryan said. "You can explain it along the way. This is getting boring."

So they started their game. Sam began by moving one of his pawns, and Ryan moved one of his. Sam realized he could capture Ryan's pawn with his knight and figured he would demonstrate what the knight could do, since Ryan hadn't wanted to learn about it before. "See?" he said, sweeping Ryan's pawn off the table. "That's one example of what the knight can do."

"Not bad," Ryan said, raising an eyebrow. Just like Nigel. He'd really have to get Nigel to teach him how to do it, Sam thought.

They continued playing, with Sam demonstrating various moves along the way, and after about twenty minutes, Ryan seemed to catch on. He captured Sam's knight and a couple of his pawns.

Mr. Alexander, who was stopping at various tables to see how everyone was doing, nodded approvingly. "Great strategy, Ryan, and Sam, you're a really good teacher." Sam smiled, a warm glow seeping through him. He valued Mr. Alexander's opinion, just as much as . . . as George Washington's, he realized. He felt the same way when George looked approvingly at him or seemed glad to see him. Of course, Mr. Alexander was here in the present time, and George was back all those years ago, but he really felt like George was a friend at this point. A friend he liked to spend time with.

"Gotcha!" Ryan shouted, taking Sam's other knight. Sam jumped, startled. "You gotta keep your mind on your game, Sam, that's always been your problem."

Sam glanced around. Mr. Alexander had moved on to another table and Ryan had the same triumphant look on his face that he did when he hit a home run in kickball or scored a goal in soccer. Well, at least I am a good teacher, Sam reflected. And I can still win this game. No more daydreaming, he told himself sternly.

But when it was time for the end of chess club, neither of them had won. Sam was impressed; Ryan had really picked up the game quickly.

"Are you sure you haven't played chess before?" Sam asked Ryan, as everyone started for the door.

"No, but my dad plays with my brother, and sometimes

I watch them," Ryan said. "That's why I'm here, okay?"

"So you can play with them, too, you mean?" Sam asked.

"So my dad will maybe finally pay some attention to me," Ryan said fiercely.

Sam tried to conjure up an image of Ryan's dad, and a burly guy wearing a Yankees baseball cap popped into his head. "Oh," Sam said. He hadn't thought much about Ryan's family before, just about Ryan's bossiness-verging-on-nastiness, and his sports ability. "You mean . . ."

"My brother gets all the attention," Ryan said. "So I'm good at sports, yeah, but he's good at sports and at everything else, too."

"Wow, that must be hard," Sam said, feeling sorry for Ryan. First Ava, now Ryan. What was going on?

"Well, maybe it turns out that I'm good at chess, too," Ryan said. He paused, and then looked at Sam. "Speaking of being good at things, do you want to hang out here at the playground? Some of the guys are playing kickball—I told them I'd show up a little late this time. I could, like, maybe give you a few pointers to help you get better at it."

Was it that obvious that he wasn't that good? Sam wondered. But it actually was kind of nice of Ryan.

"Like, Tom, Andrew, some of the others," Ryan was continuing. At the mention of Andrew's name, Sam froze. Did he really want to be out there, a not-so-good kickball and baseball player in the midst of the good players, with Andrew watching Ryan trying to help him?

After all, he hadn't played kickball or baseball or anything with these kids since last year, back when he used to be able to count on Andrew if anything went wrong. "Come on," Ryan said, grabbing Sam's arm and propelling him down the hill toward the field.

"Hey guys," Ryan said, waving at the other boys, who all stopped and looked with surprise at Sam. Andrew included, Sam noticed.

"Where were you, man?" Tom asked Ryan. "We were waiting for you, but we went ahead with the game anyway."

Ryan gave Sam a look. "Just hanging out with Sam," he said. Clearly, this chess club business was not something Tom and the others knew anything about.

"Sam, you can be on my team," Ryan announced, charging into the midst of the group as the other boys made way for him. Andrew, Sam noticed, was on the other team, headed of course by Tom. Andrew shot him a curious glance as Sam followed in Ryan's wake.

"So we're up?" Ryan asked.

"Yeah," Tom said.

As the other players prepared to kick the ball, Ryan stayed next to Sam. "Your problem is that you don't keep your focus," Ryan told Sam. "Just like back in there," and he waved toward the school building. "You pretty much let me get into the game because you weren't paying attention. When you're up, just focus on the ball, not on George Washington or anything like that."

Sam flinched. How would Ryan know that he had been thinking about George Washington? Just a lucky guess, probably. He pictured George joining in the game. Maybe standing in the outfield next to Andrew, his tall frame dwarfing the kids, even Andrew, who was pretty tall himself.

Another boy kicked the ball way out over Andrew's head. George could have caught that ball, Sam thought. It wouldn't have gone over his head. But wouldn't it be hard to play in the kind of clothes George always wore? The jackets, and then they all seemed to wear those white wigs back then? George didn't wear a wig, he knew, but a lot of others did, and . . .

"Sam, you're up!" Ryan said, giving him a shove. "See what I mean? Everyone's waiting for you!"

"Oh, right," Sam said, heading for home base. "Sorry about that."

"Pay attention to the *ball*!" Ryan yelled over to him, causing some of the other kids to snicker.

Tom, the pitcher, rolled the ball over to him, and Sam focused. It came closer, and closer, and Sam could visualize his foot coming in contact with the ball and lifting it over Andrew's head, and even over George's head, had he actually been out there. His foot connected with the ball and it skittered its way across the field, somehow finding a gap between two of the other kids. Sam made it safely to first base, feeling relieved.

"All right!" Ryan exclaimed, heading over to kick. "Now I'll get you home!"

He waited for the pitch and kicked it high into the air, over Andrew's head, halfway back to the school building. Sam took off, running around second, around third, and finally crashing into home, Ryan not far behind. "Yeah!" Ryan yelled, giving Sam a high-five. "Way to go!"

"Great kick," Sam managed, feeling a little out of breath. Just then, out of the corner of his eye, he noticed Nigel on a bench on the side of the field with some of the parents and baby sitters who had assembled, waiting to take their kids home. He was talking with Andrew's mom. Elizabeth was on the monkey bars, swinging back and forth with a couple of other girls.

Sam suddenly had a flashback to years past, when they all would have gone home together, and Sam and Andrew would have played some more, until one of the adults (or Nigel) insisted that it was time to do homework. A pang of sadness hit him in the chest as he got up.

"Not bad, Sam," Ryan said. "And thanks for the help in there."

Sam nodded. "Thank you for the help out here," he said.

Some of the adults on the bench, who had been looking at their watches, now started gathering up their kids and discussing homework and dinner. Sam made his way over to Nigel. "Can you teach me how to do that eyebrow thing?" he asked.

Nigel raised his eyebrow. "You mean this?" he inquired. "It's tricky, but I can certainly try."

Andrew's mother smiled at Sam. "Good to see you, Sam," she said, as Elizabeth ran over and started tickling him. Sam gave her a few tickles, and then looked up to find Andrew there.

"Hey, Sam," Andrew said, still looking curious. "So what were you and Ryan doing, anyway?"

Sam hesitated. In the old days, he and Andrew shared everything, but now he wasn't so sure. "Just hanging out," he said.

"But weren't you at chess club?" Andrew asked. "Or don't you do that any more?"

Sam shrugged.

"Okay," Andrew said, giving up and shifting topics. "So it was good to see you out there today. Maybe you can play kickball at recess tomorrow?"

"Maybe," Sam said, trying to seem nonchalant. "That might be good."

"Well, we need to get Elizabeth to ballet class now," said Andrew's mom, "so let's get going. Bye, Sam, bye, Nigel."

As they headed home, Sam told Nigel about Ryan and the chess club meeting. "So he wasn't so bad in the end," Sam concluded.

"Yes, you seem to have found some common ground with him," Nigel agreed. "And I'll try to teach you how to raise your eyebrow."

But when they got home, the hat was waiting for them, and it didn't seem to be in a good mood. "You're late, you're late!" it cried reproachfully from inside the Mount Vernon bag. "I had such a wonderful adventure planned for this afternoon! Where have you been, Sam?"

Sam explained. "So after chess club, I ended up playing kickball for a while," he finished.

"Ah, yes," the hat said. "I desire you in friendship, and I will one way or other make you amends."

"What?" Sam asked, confused.

"Shakespeare again?" Nigel inquired.

"But of course," the hat squeaked.

Sam frowned. "I'm not really sure what you're talking about," he said, figuring that the hat was probably trying to make another point about Andrew. "But do you still want to go on this wonderful adventure?"

"What about your homework?" Nigel said, in his role of pseudo-parent.

"Maybe the magic can work out a way that I can get back here the same time I left?" Sam asked hopefully of the hat.

"I don't know," the hat said. "I'm really not sure of that rule. Sometimes it seems to take no time at all, and other times an hour or more has passed. So I can't really promise anything."

"It probably won't take all that much time," Sam said pleadingly to Nigel.

"Well, all right, but I'm the one who's going to get in trouble when your parents come home and you're off in the eighteenth century," Nigel grumbled.

"Great!" Sam said, and he reached for the hat and put it on.

This time, the swooping feeling came over him immediately. It was strong and dizzying. He could hear people cheering and the clattering of horses and carts on, what could it be, a cobblestone street?

He opened his eyes. He was standing on a bustling

city street, outside a large building with a huge balcony, in the midst of a crowd. The people in this crowd were all looking toward the balcony. The men were wearing wigs, jackets, and knee breeches, and the women were wearing bonnets and shawls. So he was most likely in the eighteenth century, but what year? And where exactly was he?

"Three cheers for President Washington," one man shouted.

"Such an exciting day," one woman said to another. "Inauguration day at last!"

Inauguration day. Sam thought back to his classroom lessons. George had been sworn in for his first term in, what was it, 1789? And Washington, DC, still wasn't there yet, so the temporary capital at that point had been New York.

So he must be in New York City! He looked around. New York City definitely looked different from the way it appeared when Sam had gone there with his parents a year or so earlier. No tall buildings anywhere in sight. He probably should make sure, though, so he asked the two women, who were busy peering up at the balcony, exactly what was going on.

"Why, it's President Washington's inauguration!" the first woman exclaimed. "He should be arriving on the balcony soon to deliver his speech!"

"What day is it?" Sam said, wanting to be sure.

"April 30th, in the year 1789," the other woman said, seemingly hyperventilating with excitement. "A day you can tell your grandchildren about, young man."

Sam wondered if his grandchildren would believe any of this. But he thanked the women politely before trying to push his way closer toward the balcony. He had to catch George's eye.

Suddenly the crowd started to buzz with even more urgency. Sam, who had managed to make his way toward the front of the throng, saw a group of men assembling on the balcony. He peered up and there was George, a solemn expression on his face, surrounded by equally solemn-looking men. This was serious stuff, Sam thought, a really big deal. Inaugurating the very first president of a new country.

One of the men handed George a Bible, and George, dressed in a brown suit, began to take the oath of office, repeating the words after the man had spoken them. What must be going on in George's head right now? Sam wondered.

". . . that I will faithfully execute the office of President of the United States . . ." George was saying.

Sam shifted around to get a better view. He wished the hat had landed him up on the balcony, but at least he had been able to get fairly close so he could see what was going on. He'd have to figure out a way to get up there once the ceremony was done.

"Long live George Washington, President of the United States," the man next to George on the balcony called out, and cannons began to fire as the crowd cheered. Sam found himself cheering, too. This was incredible!

But then the group of men, George among them, started to head back inside. Sam really wanted to go in there with them, and he sent some thought waves toward the hat, not that thought waves had ever helped before.

He really had to get to see George and congratulate him. But could he push his way into the building? All he could do was try. Gradually, he maneuvered around the cheering masses of people and past some uniformed soldiers, and found a door, which was slightly open. He slipped inside.

It seemed hushed and quiet compared to the noise on the street. But he could hear a hum of voices coming from somewhere above. He found his way to a staircase and crept into a large, ornate room. George was standing at the front, apparently about to start making a speech— his inaugural address, Sam presumed.

Sam pressed against one of the walls, hoping no one would notice him. There were no other kids in the room.

As the crowd quieted down, George, who actually looked a little nervous for the first time since Sam had met him, began to speak.

"Fellow Citizens of the Senate and the House of Representatives," George said. "Among the vicissitudes incident to life, no event could have filled me with greater anxieties than that of which the notification was transmitted by your order, and received on the fourteenth day of the present month."

That must have been the notice from Congress that they wanted him to be president, Sam thought, amazed that George would admit to being anxious. But it definitely made him seem more human, more like a real person.

As George continued speaking, Sam looked around the room to see if he could recognize anyone else, and he paused at one familiar figure. He was short and had a roundish face and a sharp nose.

Was that John Adams? He must have just been sworn in as vice president. Sam had learned something about John Adams at school, and what immediately came to mind was that he was married to Abigail Adams, that he was the first vice president and the second president, and that he wasn't as popular as George Washington.

As he looked at John Adams, something seemed to shimmer next to the vice president. Two things, one on each side of him.

Sam shook his head as if to clear it. What were those shimmering shapes? For some reason, Ava and J. P.

popped into his head. But why would he be thinking of them? What did they have to do with John Adams, anyway, except that Ava had written her book report about Abigail?

Still, he found that he couldn't take his eyes off the shimmering forms next to John Adams. Was this part of the magic, too? Stop it, he told himself. You really should be focusing on what George is saying, and not on something that might well be just a trick of the light. He managed to pull his gaze from the shimmering forms and back to George, who seemed to be in the concluding phase of his speech.

"Having thus imported to you my sentiments, as they have been awakened by the occasion which brings us together, I shall take my present leave," George said, "but not without resorting once more to the benign parent of the human race, in humble supplication that since he has been pleased to favor the American people, with opportunities for deliberating in perfect tranquility, and dispositions for deciding with unparalleled unanimity on a form of Government, for the security of their Union, and the advancement of their happiness; so his divine blessing may be equally conspicuous in the enlarged views, the temperate consultations, and the wise measures on which the success of this Government must depend."

At this point, George drew a deep breath and stopped speaking. In the hubbub that ensued, Sam managed to push his way toward George, who of course was surrounded by well-wishers, including vice president Adams.

The two shimmering forms glided toward Sam, who began to feel nervous. What did they want, anyway? One of them, which was about his height, reached out and touched his arm, and the other one, a little smaller, seemed to be gesturing at him. But he couldn't tell, because the light surrounding them hurt his eyes, and the two forms looked kind of blurry and out of focus.

At that moment, George, who must have just caught sight of Sam, advanced upon him, and the two shimmering forms returned to John Adams, one on either side of him. One of the forms, the smaller one, seemed as if it wanted to stay near Sam, but the other one pulled it toward John Adams, and then the first one seemed to shrug, but Sam couldn't tell. And anyway, he wanted to talk to George, not deal with some weird apparitions.

"Sam, how wonderful that you could be here," George said, shaking Sam's hand enthusiastically.

"Congratulations, sir, I mean, Mr. President," Sam said, his attention back on George. "This was really amazing!"

"It was not my finest speech," George said, shaking his head. "I fear I was somewhat overcome by nerves and emotion. You know, Sam, it was my dream to spend some quiet years with Martha at Mount Vernon. The country has been through so much, and I do admit to feeling tired at times. But when the Congress summoned me, I felt that I must once more serve my country."

"Of course," Sam said encouragingly. "And you are the true father of our country. That's how you'll be known to schoolchildren for hundreds of years!"

George looked a little skeptical. "If you say so, Sam," George said. "You know I have always valued your opinion, ever since we first met back at Mount Vernon. You have been a true and loyal friend."

"Thank you, Mr. President," Sam said, finding that he was blinking away some tears. "I feel the same way about you. I mean, I've always looked up to you, but since I've gotten to know you, I really feel like we're friends."

George nodded kindly.

"And I had this one friend, and we're not really friends any more, but getting to know you has really made me feel a lot better about things," Sam babbled on, not having planned to say any of this at all, indeed, not really having thought any of it out before. It was all just pouring out of him. "It's been so great spending all this time with you, even though I always wish I could stay for longer. And . . ."

Just then, a couple of men pushed toward George, beaming and reaching out to shake George's hand and clap him on the back.

"Sam," George called out to him from over the heads of the two men, "I do hope you can stay longer this time and perhaps join us in some of our celebrations?"

"I hope so, too," Sam said.

The two men turned toward Sam, and one of them doffed his hat to Sam. Sam, instinctively trying to be polite, did the same.

And then the room faded away and he was standing inside the front hallway of his house. "Oh, no!" Sam said, frustrated beyond words.

"I know you were trying to be polite," the hat said squeakily. It was still in his hand. "But you must know by now that I must remain on your head!"

"Yes, I know," Sam said, heaving a sigh. He could hear his parents in the kitchen and Nigel's footsteps bolting up from the basement. "I'm really relieved you're back," Nigel said. "I told your parents you were over at Ava and J. P.'s house, but dinner's almost ready, and I knew Aunt Melissa would be calling over there for you."

Yes, Sam was sure his mom would indeed have done that, and soon, too. Because he could smell the aroma of a chicken dinner wafting in from the kitchen and could hear the sounds of plates and glasses being set on the table. It's funny that Nigel would have thought of Ava and J. P., right when Sam was thinking of them, too.

"So what happened? Where did you go this time?" Nigel asked. Sam was about to answer when he heard his mom's voice.

"Nigel? Would you mind running across the street and telling Sam to come back for dinner? I'm just taking this chicken out of the oven, and Uncle Phil's busy with the salad."

"I'm already here, Mom," Sam said, putting the hat back in the Mount Vernon bag. As Sam was about to head into the kitchen, the hat gave its now-familiar wink.

The day of the play arrived, and the level of excitement and jangled nerves had been rising all morning in Ms. Martin's classroom. Oliver seemed to be in his own world, his mouth moving. Most likely practicing his lines, Sam figured. Sam's own lines consisted of "Very good, General," and "Yes, sir," so he didn't have a whole lot to practice.

Sam, behind the curtain with his classmates, could hear the noise of the younger grades sitting down in the all-purpose room to watch the first performance of the play. His class would perform the George Washington play, and the other two fifth-grade classes would each perform their own play, one about Benjamin Franklin and one about King George III. A second show would follow in the evening for parents.

The hat, ensconced on Sam's head, was behaving beautifully. It wasn't sending Sam back to the eighteenth century. It wasn't complaining about anything. It wasn't even talking. Sam had given it strict instructions before leaving for school that morning, warning the hat that if it was going to come along, it would need to abide by certain rules of conduct.

"Good luck, everyone," Ms. Martin said as she began to pull the curtain open. "I know you'll do a fabulous job!"

Sam felt the old familiar rush of appearing on stage sweep over him. It didn't matter, really, that he only had two lines. It still was a thrill to be up there. He watched as Oliver went up on stage, and then the other kids playing their parts, and suddenly he and his fellow soldiers were up there, and he was saying, "Very good, General," and "Yes, sir," and in what seemed like only a few minutes, the play was over and he and his fellow cast members came out for a curtain call, before ceding the stage to the Benjamin Franklin cast members.

"Wonderful, wonderful!" Ms. Martin was saying, bustling around backstage and congratulating her students. "Tonight will be just as good, even better!"

Soon enough, it was time for recess and lunch. Much to Sam's surprise, Ryan, followed by Tom and Andrew, approached him as the class was heading out to the playground.

"You want to play today?" Ryan inquired, poking Sam in the arm. "I'm thinking we'll switch from kickball and play soccer."

"Yeah, okay," Sam said, experiencing a combination of puzzlement—why was Ryan doing this?—and relief—now he, Sam, wouldn't have to wander around looking pitiful during recess.

Ryan nodded and immediately began discussing with Tom which kids would play on each of their respective teams. Andrew, somewhat left out of the discussion, drifted next to Sam.

"Hey," Andrew said. "So what have you been up to lately, anyway? I haven't seen you around much."

"Well, you're the one who's not around," Sam burst out, unable to stop himself. "You're always playing baseball, or spending time with them," and he gestured toward Ryan and Tom, who had jogged ahead and down to the field.

"Well, I can't help that!" Andrew said. "I asked you if you wanted to do all those baseball clinics last year, and you said no, you'd rather just ride around on your bike."

By this point, they had reached the field. Ryan and Tom, and a group of other kids, had started kicking the ball around, but Sam wasn't interested at this point.

"I didn't say that," Sam said, stung. Had he? He had wanted to spend time riding his bike, yes, but wasn't it more that he just didn't feel like he was that good at baseball and didn't want to devote so much effort to it? Suddenly he felt as if he might start to cry. But that couldn't happen, not here, not now. It would be too embarrassing.

"Andrew?" Ryan called.

"Go ahead without me," Andrew called over. A muscle in his cheek was twitching a little, which Sam knew meant that Andrew was really upset. He turned back to Sam. "I really tried. But you didn't seem to want to hang out any more."

"I didn't?" Sam said, feeling as if he would lose the battle against the tears. "No, it's you who didn't!" Pull yourself together, he told himself. Pretend you're up on stage. Pretend you're George. "You're never around any more."

"And this whole obsession you have with George Washington?" Andrew continued, as if somehow sensing what Sam was thinking. "How do you know all those things about what he thinks, or what he did, or how he walks around, or whatever?"

Sam was startled. He could hear a little gasp coming from the hat, which was still on his head.

"Obsession?" he managed.

"Yeah," Andrew said.

Sam stopped and thought. Maybe he should just tell Andrew the whole thing, as he would have in the past. But he was swamped with the same sensation he'd had the day before, when Andrew had asked him what was going on with Ryan. Things had changed from the way they always used to be. And he didn't really want to say anything now.

"I've just been reading a lot about him," he said. "He was an interesting guy."

Andrew shrugged. "Okay," he said. And he turned and ran over to join the soccer players.

Sam didn't feel like playing soccer. He didn't feel like doing anything much, except maybe going home and curling up in a corner.

"Isn't it possible," the hat suddenly said in its squeaky voice, "that Andrew's feeling unhappy too? Perhaps he misses you as much as you miss him."

"I doubt that," Sam muttered, kicking at a clump of grass.

"It would be wise to consider the other perspective," the hat said, before lapsing into silence once more.

Consider the other perspective? Why should he do that? Andrew had abandoned him for baseball and for Ryan and Tom, and that was the story. But then the image of Andrew's twitching cheek popped into Sam's mind. Andrew really had been upset. And this cast some doubt on the narrative that Sam had been telling himself for months.

He paused. Could the hat have a point? Maybe Andrew felt as bad about things as Sam did. Maybe Sam really had given the impression that he'd rather just ride around on his bike than spend time with Andrew. Maybe . . .

"Ha! Caught you!" Samantha was suddenly in front of him, Ava at her side. "Lost in thought again!"

"Yeah, I guess so," Sam said, switching his focus to the two of them and feeling oddly glad to see them. Their best-friend bond didn't seem to waver. Maybe it was a good omen: that friendship could in fact last. He wondered . . . "Have you guys ever had a fight?" he asked. "Like, a big fight when you didn't talk to each other for a while?"

Ava and Samantha exchanged glances, as if they knew what he was really getting at. They undoubtedly had seen him talking with Andrew and would probably be sitting out on Ava's porch swing later, speculating about what was going on.

"Well, there was that time back in third grade," Ava said, squinting thoughtfully. "Remember, Samantha? It had to do with Katie. She told you that I didn't want to be friends with you any more, and you actually believed her."

Samantha nodded. "Yeah, I should have just asked you, but I felt weird about it, and it took a while to get the whole thing cleared up."

At that point, the recess aides began blowing whistles and beckoning the kids to line up for lunch. Sam followed Ava and Samantha into the cafeteria. "I should have just asked you," Samantha had said. Should he have asked Andrew how he was really feeling? Should Andrew have asked him?

The rest of the school day passed in a blur, and before he knew it, it was time to go home. Sam and the hat, which had remained remarkably quiet since recess, got on the bus. Oliver sat down next to him. "Nice job,

Oliver," Sam said, snapping out of his reverie and focusing on Oliver, who after all had done well as George.

"Thanks," Oliver said, sounding pleased. "Now we just have to get through tonight's performance. My parents and my sisters are all going to be there. You know, I've never been the star of a play before, and they're all kind of wondering if I really can do it. Even though I've been practicing a lot at home and all."

"Well, I thought it was quite good," the hat suddenly piped up from atop Sam's head. "There were a few times when I thought you captured General Washington's gestures very well."

Oliver looked startled. Fortunately, the bus was noisy with the sounds of kids' conversations, so no one else seemed to hear. "Was that you, Sam?" he asked. "You really are good at acting! That didn't sound like your normal voice at all!"

Sam adopted an expression that he hoped looked modest. "Well, I've been working on different voices, accents, you know."

The bus jerked to a halt at the playground, and Sam, relieved, jumped to his feet and followed Oliver off the bus. He couldn't wait to get home and have a couple of hours to relax before heading back to school for the evening's performance. Maybe discuss the Andrew situation with Nigel.

But Oliver once again opted to follow Sam in the direction of Sam's house. Sam sent some thought waves to the hat, begging it to remain silent until Oliver was out of the vicinity.

But the hat, apparently liberated from its promise to be quiet around other people, didn't comply. It cleared its throat and spoke up again. "I said, that was a good performance, young man." By this point, Sam and Oliver had made it down the block.

"Wow, Sam, I really like that voice," Oliver said. "That was a good performance, young man," he mimicked, in a high-pitched tone.

"Well, really!" the hat said indignantly.

"Well, really!" Oliver mimicked.

"I don't care for this!" the hat said.

"I don't care for this!" Oliver said.

Sam rolled his eyes. "Oliver, I need to get going now," he said, not sure how much longer this bizarre conversation could, or should, continue.

"What about if I come over to your house?" Oliver said.

"I kind of have some stuff to do," Sam said.

"What stuff?" Oliver inquired.

"You know, helping my cousin with some projects," Sam improvised.

The hat, tired of being ignored, jumped into the discussion. "Sam, did you ever consider crossing the Delaware?"

"What?" Sam said, confused.

"Did you ever consider crossing the Delaware?" Oliver mimicked.

"All these wonderful events in the play, and I must say, the most dramatic moment was the crossing of the Delaware," the hat continued.

"The most dramatic moment was the crossing of the Delaware," Oliver parroted.

"Oliver, could you stop that, please?" Sam said, fed up. "I want to hear this."

"But you're the one saying it," Oliver said, confused. "Why do you need to hear it?"

"Sam's not saying it," the hat said, sounding upset. "I'm saying it." And it jumped up and down on Sam's head.

Oliver looked even more confused. "Your hat's moving up and down," he pointed out. "And how do you do that voice without even moving your mouth?" He reached out for the hat, and Sam reached up to hold it down on his head, and suddenly the swirling feeling came over him, right there on the street corner a couple of blocks from his house.

And then, of course, the street corner wasn't there any more, and instead he—oh, no, with Oliver!—was standing in a frozen field. It was dusk. He could hear the shouts of men in the distance and a noise that sounded like rushing water.

"Whoa!" Oliver screamed. "What's going on? Where am I? What happened? Where's our neighborhood?"

"I think we're about to experience the crossing of the Delaware," Sam said, feeling a sense of trepidation. What was the hat doing? Why had it brought Oliver along?

"December 1776," Oliver said, his genius-like qualities apparently overcoming his fear. "George Washington's surprise attack by night against the Hessian troops across the river in New Jersey." And he struck a George-like pose, imitating the famous painting showing the crossing of the Delaware. "But wait a minute. I don't understand!"

"Okay," Sam said. He figured he should tell the whole thing. "So this is a magic hat. I got it last week at the Mount Vernon gift shop. Ever since then, it's been sending me back to George Washington's time, and I've gotten to meet him and talk to him, and spend time with him."

"You have?" Oliver said. "But I'm the one who's playing him! Why didn't this happen to me?"

"I have no idea," Sam said, feeling impatient. "The point is that you happened to be there when the hat decided to take me back here, so we're both here. And now we need to look for George."

"First-name basis?" Oliver said. "That sounds good to me! So where do we find him?"

"We'll find him, don't worry," Sam said. But he was puzzled about something. So far, the hat had taken him chronologically through George's life, from a teenager to a young man to a general to the president. Now, all of a sudden, they were back in 1776. Why? And of course the hat had become silent, as it did during these visits, so there was no way to find out.

"Let's head that way," Sam said, pointing toward a group of men and horses gathered far across the field. The two of them started moving forward. The frozen earth crunched under their feet. Sam looked up. The sky was grayish-black and a few flakes of snow drifted down. Sam shivered.

"I'm cold," Oliver whined. "Doesn't this magic hat provide coats?"

"Not really," Sam said. "But I don't usually feel it that much. Maybe you'll get used to it."

They marched onward and eventually came closer to the men. In the same ragged attire Sam had seen at Valley Forge—although this was a year earlier—the men were gesturing toward what must be the Delaware River. The water looked angry, swirling around in white-capped waves.

"Boys, can you give us a hand?" one soldier called, and Sam sprinted toward him, followed more slowly by Oliver. Sam joined the soldier and a few other men who were loading some supplies onto a ferryboat moored at the landing. Oliver stood beside the boat as everyone else worked.

"What's going on here, anyway?" Oliver asked. "Where's the general? I'd kind of like to meet him."

"Why don't you help?" Sam huffed and puffed at Oliver. "Don't just stand there."

Oliver ignored him. "Wow, that water looks really cold!" he said, moving ahead of Sam and the others toward the icy Delaware.

"It's dark, and soon the crossing begins," the soldier told Sam. "The Durham boats should be arriving soon. We'll take those Hessians by surprise." He started coughing, and once his coughs had subsided, he continued. "Odd way to spend my Christmas, but I think the general has a good plan."

"Yes, he does," Sam said. "You will be successful, I know it."

"Well, thank ye kindly, young man," the soldier said, his narrow face brightening. "For your encouragement, and for helping."

"Oh, you're very welcome," Sam said.

"My name's Hezekiah," the soldier said.

"Sam," Sam replied. Just as he was about to ask Hezekiah some more questions—where he was from, what he thought of his fellow troops—Oliver reappeared.

"So where is he?" he demanded. "If I'm playing him, I really want to meet him!"

"Do you know where General Washington might be?" Sam inquired of Hezekiah.

"Over yonder," Hezekiah answered, gesturing to the left. Sam thanked him, and, Oliver in tow, started searching for George. As they walked in the direction Hezekiah had indicated, Sam glanced around at the troops, noticing that a number of them were African-American. He wondered if they were slaves or if they were free.

"It's snowing!" Oliver announced, and sure enough, wet flakes were descending around them. "Come on, where is he? I'm cold!"

Honestly, Oliver was really getting on Sam's nerves. "We'll find him, okay?" Sam answered. "I always find him on these trips."

They walked on, and then, "There he is!" Oliver cried, pointing ahead. "He looks just like I imagined!"

Sure enough, there was George, wrapped in a blue

and red cloak. He was wearing tan breeches, black knee-high boots, and a black hat. As usual, he was surrounded by a group of soldiers and seemed deep in conversation.

Oliver rushed forward, apparently not caring if he was interrupting. "General Washington!" he proclaimed. "At last! I have the honor of portraying you in my school play!"

George turned, a puzzled look on his face. "Portraying me? In a school play?"

"Yes!" Oliver announced. "We're from the twenty-first . . ."

"Hello, General Washington," Sam burst in, cutting Oliver off. For some reason, he didn't want George to know that he, Sam, was from another century.

"Ah, Sam!" George said, bestowing a smile on Sam. "Wonderful! And this is a friend of yours?"

"Oliver, General Washington," Sam said, making the introduction.

"You've caught me at a rather busy time," George said. "As darkness is now upon us, we are about to make ready to cross the Delaware. You will ride with me in my boat?"

"Of course," Sam said. He wondered if the artist who painted the famous picture of George crossing the Delaware could add in a couple more figures.

"This snow could cause problems," George said thoughtfully, looking at the sky. The flakes were coming down harder now, and the winds were picking up, causing the snow to swirl faster.

"Naah, you'll make it just fine," Oliver said. "No problem."

George looked at Sam. "Do you agree?" he asked.

"Yes, I do," Sam said. "It will be viewed by historians as one of the turning points of the war, I'm sure."

George nodded, clapping Sam on the back. "It's always a tonic to my spirits to see you, Sam!" he exclaimed.

"General Washington." One of George's fellow soldiers was coming up behind him. "We need your counsel on some matters involving the horses."

"Excuse me for a moment, Sam," George said. "And Oliver. I will see you shortly." And he moved away with his colleague.

"Wow," Oliver said. "This is too cool! I can't believe this! I need to take some mental notes to help with my performance tonight! Do you want to act out a scene with me now? The one where we cross the Delaware?"

Sam agreed. Why not? So the two of them took their positions, pretending to be in a boat. Oliver, playing George, issued orders, and Sam, playing a soldier, said, "Very good, General."

"And what are you doing?" George said, taking them by surprise. He had a twinkle in his eye.

"We're acting it out," Oliver said self-importantly. "The crossing."

"Of course," George said. "Well, the time has come."

"The real crossing?" Oliver asked.

"That very one," George said. Indeed, a series of boats floated along the river's edge. Officers were barking orders and the rank and file were obeying. Just like in the play, Sam thought.

"General?" one of the men said from the ferry landing, indicating that George should enter the boat. George ushered Sam and Oliver into the boat before stepping in himself.

The boat bobbed on the water as the men pushed off. Sam could hear someone, an officer, no doubt, calling out some instructions, but he couldn't make out exactly what he was saying. George seemed lost in thought. For the most part, everyone was silent.

"Ice floe up ahead," one of the men said in a hushed tone, gesturing.

"We must go around it," George said in a near-whisper. "See, those other boats ahead have done the same thing."

The boat began rocking harder with the wind, and Sam felt a little queasy. The men with the oars were sweating, despite the cold. George seemed unperturbed. "Onward," he said, quietly but firmly. "Courage."

The boat plowed onward. Sam could see other boats making their way around the ice. With the snow cutting down on visibility, he couldn't see much beyond the few boats that were closest to them.

"How long will the crossing take?" he whispered to George.

Just then, Oliver groaned. "I think I'm going to throw up!" he announced loudly, and he stood up, preparing to lean over the side of the boat. A gust of wind hit the vessel and Oliver toppled out, into the icy water. "Help!" he shrieked. Sam gasped. He reached out to try to help him, as did George and the other men. Somehow, in all the tumult, as a shivering, blubbering Oliver was pulled back into the boat, Sam's hat fell off.

And a second later, Sam was back on the street corner in his neighborhood. But Oliver wasn't there. And neither was Sam's hat.

Chapter ~8~

Sam looked around. Definitely no Oliver. And definitely no hat. He looked around again. Maybe the hat was somewhere nearby, a couple of houses away, having fallen off in the journey back to the present? Maybe Oliver was hiding behind a tree? "Oliver?" he called out. He wasn't exactly sure how to address the hat, as he had never had to call for it before. "Hat?" he asked tentatively.

But there was no reply. He started looking up and down the street for the hat. "Hat?" he called out. "Hat?" Nothing. Sam started to panic. Where was the hat? And where was Oliver? What was going on? "Hat?" he cried, louder now. "Hat?" If Oliver and the hat were back in the eighteenth century, how on earth would they get home? Oliver didn't know how the hat operated, and the hat never said anything helpful, or anything at all, when it was back in the past. And how could Sam get back there again without the hat on his head? "Hat!" he bellowed. "Hat!"

A vaguely familiar-looking lady from the neighborhood jogged by. "I saw a cat down that way," she said, pointing behind her. "Gray with a little white? Maybe that was your cat?"

Sam saw no need to correct her. "Thank you," he said as she headed up the street. If he even had a cat, which he didn't, why would it be named "cat" anyway? That wasn't very imaginative. But she had only been trying to help. He paused for a minute, imagining that he was in fact looking for a cat. A cat would have an idea of how to get home. Would the hat somehow be able to get Oliver back home without Sam there?

He needed some help, that was clear, and Nigel was the best option. "Nigel," he cried, bursting into the house a few minutes later. "I don't know what to do!"

Nigel emerged from his basement lair. "What happened?" he exclaimed, looking alarmed. "You look dreadful. Things didn't go well with the play?"

"No, it isn't that," Sam

said. "The play was fine. It's what happened afterwards!" And he told Nigel about it.

Nigel looked grave. "So Oliver is back there in George's boat crossing the Delaware, and the hat is there, too?"

"If it didn't fall in the river," Sam said, that possibility dawning on him. "I think it was still in the boat, but it was pretty windy and the waves were kind of high." He paused, thinking back on the scene. "Oliver knows the hat is magic," he added. "I told him about it. So I expect he'll take good care of it."

"Well, that's good," Nigel said. "But Oliver doesn't always seem to have a lot of common sense."

Just then, the phone rang and Sam answered it. Speaking of Oliver . . .

"Sam? It's Cassie. Oliver's sister. We thought maybe you would know where he is. He hasn't come home yet."

Sam gulped. What on earth should he tell her?

"Sam?" Cassie's voice came through loudly. "Sam?"

"Uh, yeah, he's with me," Sam said. Then he stopped. Why had he said that? What if she needed him home right then? What would he say?

"Great!" Cassie said, sounding relieved. "He can stay there for a while, that's fine, he just needs to get home by dinner time. Can I talk to him for a second?"

Not really, Sam thought. Now what should I do?

"Sam?" Cassie said. "Oh, that's okay, just tell him to be home by dinner time. Thanks!" And she hung up.

Sam sighed. He looked at his watch. 3:30. At least he had a while before Oliver needed to get home and get ready for dinner and the evening performance of the play.

"So we have a couple of hours," Nigel said, having heard Cassie's voice through the receiver. "Let me call Celia and see if she had any ideas." He pulled out his cell phone, and a moment later, having put her on speakerphone, was filling her in on the day's events.

Sam, half-listening to them, was trying to figure out what to do. Clearly, he needed to get back to the Delaware, retrieve Oliver and the hat, and get them back in time for dinner. But how could he get there without the hat? Maybe there were other hats in the Mount Vernon gift shop, even if they weren't magic ones. Could the magic have rubbed off on them? But it was getting close to rush hour and the traffic would be backing up, and how could he get to Mount Vernon in time? The gift shop would probably be closed by then anyway.

What about a picture of George crossing the Delaware? He rushed over to the computer and searched. Immediately, a page of photos, mostly of the famous painting of the crossing, popped up on the screen. George's hat in that picture wasn't much like the magic hat, but it was worth a try.

"Oh, hat," Sam said, focusing all his energy on the hat in the image on the screen. "Oh, hat, please get me back to the crossing of the Delaware. Please let me get my hat back and rescue Oliver." He closed his eyes. But nothing happened. He was still sitting in front of the computer.

It had to be something that actually looked like the magic hat and had a connection to George. Something had to work. It was his responsibility to retrieve Oliver and bring him home.

Statues! There must be some images of George around the DC area. After all, it had been named for him. Maybe even at George Washington University. He searched again on the computer, and a series of statues of George popped up. Only one of them seemed to have a hat like Sam's, though. This statue was located at the Washington National Cathedral.

"Okay, here's an idea," Nigel said, coming up behind Sam and startling him. "The Racing Presidents. You know, from the Nats games."

The Racing Presidents were a group of huge, mascot-like figures with massive, cartoon-like heads. They were named for George and other long-ago presidents. At each Washington Nationals home game, the presidents raced one another around the baseball field in the middle of the fourth inning.

"Yes!" Sam said. "And there's a Nats game today, so maybe we can find George in the stadium! And here's another idea." He showed Nigel the picture of the George statue at the National Cathedral.

"I'm not sure how we'll get to all these places that quickly," Nigel said, "but Celia's coming by now with her car, so she can drive us and drop us off if need be."

Moments later, the three of them were in Celia's car, an ancient vehicle that seemed about to give up its last breath. "It's old, but it goes," Celia said cheerfully as she pushed down on the accelerator, causing the car to wheeze slightly. "So first stop, Cathedral?"

"Yes," Sam said. "And thanks, Celia." She did seem incredibly helpful, Sam reflected as the car bounced along. He hoped Celia would end up being Nigel's girlfriend. Maybe one day they would get married and Celia would be his cousin-in-law. Maybe they would move back to London, and one day Sam would go there and live with them. Maybe . . .

His thoughts were interrupted by the car screeching to a halt. The cathedral loomed next to them. "I'll be here waiting," Celia said, as Nigel and Sam leaped out of the car and rushed toward the massive building. Located on a high point of the city, the cathedral, with its tall spires, could be seen from quite a distance away. Sam had never been inside it. "Do you know where this statue is?" he asked Nigel as they approached an entrance.

"I think so," Nigel said. "Celia looked it up online."

They made their way inside and down a couple of dark stone hallways, and there, indeed, was a large statue of George, holding a hat that looked just like Sam's. Sam smiled in recognition. Surely this would work.

He looked at the cold stone hat. "Oh, hat," he said, wishing with all his might. "Oh, hat, please get me back to the crossing of the Delaware. I really need to rescue my hat, and rescue Oliver, too. His family will be so worried about him, and it will all be my fault. Please, oh, hat."

Nothing.

What if he touched the hat? Sam looked around. No one else was nearby; it was just Sam and Nigel in the cool shadowy space. Would an alarm go off? Well, it was worth trying. The stakes were high enough. He climbed onto the statue, shimmied up, and grabbed onto the hat. "Oh, hat," he said once more. No alarms were sounding, so that was good. "Please take me to the crossing of the Delaware. Please, oh, hat."

The hat began to feel hot to the touch, but Sam held on. A dizzy feeling hit him, but it wasn't the same as the feeling when he put on his own magic hat. It was choppy and bouncy. Kind of like how it felt in the boat crossing the Delaware. Was that a good sign?

Feeling a little sick, Sam closed his eyes, only to find himself bounced, hard, on the ground. He opened his eyes. He wasn't in the cathedral any more, but instead on an embankment. A river was flowing in front of him. Was it the Delaware? This couldn't be right. The weather was warm and humid, just as it had been back home, and the sun was shining. No snow. No cold. There were buildings near the shore that hadn't been there before and a set of cement steps led down to the river. Those certainly hadn't been there before. And just then, a group of people approached him. He squinted at them. Modern clothes. What was going on?

"And from this site, the boats set out," a man's voice rang out. Sam looked up. "This is one of the high points of our tour, folks! It was cold, the snow was beginning, and the men were shivering." The man chuckled. "Hard to imagine on a day like today, right?"

Not really, Sam thought, his mind flashing back to George and the soldiers in their boats.

"Are you joining our tour, young man?" the man, who

Sam realized must be some sort of tour guide leading a group, inquired.

Sam stood up. "Um, yes, I think so."

People were pulling out their cell phones and taking pictures of the river.

Oh, no. The stone hat had tried its best, but this was completely wrong. Here Sam was, at the crossing, but it was still the twenty-first century. And now how would he get back?

The guide was telling the group about George's bravery and the successful surprise attack on the Hessians in New Jersey, but Sam couldn't concentrate. He needed to get back home. Now.

He closed his eyes and pictured George wearing the hat. "Oh, hat, oh, George, if you can hear me, please help me! I need to get myself back to Nigel. Right now! Please? Hat? Please?"

Sam felt himself begin to shake all over, and once more he closed his eyes, and there he was, back in the National Cathedral with Nigel, next to the stone statue of George. He breathed a sigh of relief.

Nigel looked astonished. "Extraordinary!" he exclaimed. "But where's the hat? And where's Oliver?"

Sam explained.

"On to Nats Park!" Nigel cried, and the two of them rushed back to Celia's car.

"The traffic will be awful, so I'll drop you at the Metro," Celia announced, flooring the pedal on her car, which shot forward, heading toward the Metro stop.

The trip to Nationals Park involved a change from the

Red Line to the Green Line, but the trains were running pretty often, it being rush hour, so before long, Sam and Nigel were heading toward the Nationals ticket office.

Nigel checked the time. "We still have about an hour," he said, "before Oliver's family starts to call and wonder where he is."

Sam loved coming to Nats games. Despite his worry over Oliver and the hat, he felt a sense of excitement as he and Nigel entered the gates and joined the fans, mostly clad in red, trickling in for the game.

There weren't many people there yet, so Sam began scouring the curving concourse for George or one of the other Racing Presidents. The huge field looked green and peaceful and the lines at the food stalls were short. But there was no time to reflect on that. Sam had to find George. Immediately. Nigel, he noticed, was bent over his phone, busily texting. Probably to Celia, Sam figured.

Sam approached one of the food vendors. "Have you seen George?" he inquired. "The racing president?"

"No," the man answered, "But I saw Abe a minute ago. Heading that way." The Abraham Lincoln figure. Sam and Nigel, looking up from his phone, hurried in that direction. Maybe Abe knew where George was.

Sure enough, the looming figure of Abe could be seen in the distance, and Sam and Nigel broke into a run.

"Abe!" Sam called. "Abe?"

The figure, with its massive head, turned around slowly.

"Have you seen George? We need to find him."

The Abe figure turned slowly and pointed up a level. Maybe these figures couldn't talk? Sam wondered. Or the people who were inside them weren't allowed to? He and Nigel thanked Abe and raced to the upper deck.

They started running to the right and soon spotted another huge head, this time with a wig and pony tail. "George!" Sam shouted. "George!"

George, who had just finished having his picture taken with a couple of kids, turned toward Sam and Nigel. Sam explained the whole story as the figure stood impassively. I guess they don't talk, Sam thought. But I hope they can listen!

"But Sam," Nigel said, interrupting. "I just realized—George isn't wearing a hat!"

Sam stopped, crestfallen. Nigel was right. None of the Racing Presidents had hats. But at least this was George, and maybe just being with something resembling George, hat or no hat, would be useful.

The figure reached out for Sam's hand, and Sam took it and began wishing again. "Oh, George, oh, hat, please help me rescue Oliver!" A shudder ran through him at the thought of Oliver, trapped forever back in the eighteenth century with no way home. "Please, George, please, hat, I really need to get back there." And despite Sam's efforts to avoid it, a tear trickled down his cheek. Nigel reached out for Sam, and suddenly Sam felt everything spinning around, and he and George and Nigel seemed to float up into the air, and then they landed with a thud.

The river was in front of them. It was the same place Sam had been earlier, and it was still warm outside. The buildings and the cement steps were still there. In the distance, Sam could see another tour guide leading a group in their direction. So now what? He was at the Delaware again, but still in the present day with no sense of how to get back to December 1776.

Then George pointed and bobbed his huge head out in the direction of the river. He started toward the water, and soon he was swimming along, his giant head floating on the surface. It would have been funny if Sam hadn't been so worried.

Nigel was looking around, his eyes popping. Of course, this was the first time he had been transported anywhere, Sam realized. He patted his cousin on the shoulder. "It's okay," he said. "We're at the Delaware. I think we're still in the present day, though."

Nigel was shivering, despite the warmth. "All right," he said, his teeth chattering. "Maybe we need to follow George? He seems to have some ideas."

Maybe George was heading into the water because that's where the hat had fallen from Sam's head? "Yes, let's try it," he cried, and he and Nigel ran down the steps and into the water. It was cold, but not too bad once they got used to it, and soon they were swimming along, their shorts and T-shirts clinging to them.

George's big head bobbed along in front of them, and suddenly he pointed to a spot just ahead. Gesturing to Sam and Nigel, he indicated that the three of them should join hands and form a circle, which they did.

And then, although the river had been fairly calm, a wave suddenly appeared and crashed over them, and

Sam coughed and spluttered and closed his eyes and felt the water rush past. And then he heard a voice. An annoying voice, but one of the most welcome sounds he had ever heard.

"Sam," the voice said. It sounded raspy. "Where did you go? I was wondering if maybe you had a cough lozenge or something like that. I know George and his men wouldn't have anything, even though they all seem to have a cough, because I don't think lozenges had been invented yet."

Sam opened his eyes. There he was, back in the boat, the snow coming down, and Oliver was next to him, wearing the hat. Sam was so excited, he couldn't help it—he threw his arms around Oliver, who promptly sneezed all over him.

"Oh, sorry," Oliver said, coughing. He looked wet and cold. "Hey, here's your hat."

Sam didn't even mind about the sneeze. He popped the hat, which seemed to wink at him, back on his own head, and a sense of calm and relief settled over him.

"Glad to have you back on board, Sam," said George. The real George, not the mascot. "We weren't sure where you went, but I told the men, and Oliver here, that you always turn up again."

"Yes, I do," Sam said, smiling happily at the lot of them.

"Hey, Sam, I think I'm coming down with something," Oliver said. Sam could see that he was shivering, sort of like Nigel had back on the shore. Oliver coughed again.

Sam had to get Oliver home, that was clear. The boats

were approaching the New Jersey shore, and George was huddling with his men, making plans.

"My sisters probably are wondering where I am," Oliver rasped. He sounded like he was coming down with laryngitis.

"Yeah, Cassie called and I told her you were with me." Sam remembered the phone call, and figuring out what to do, and discussing it with Nigel, and suddenly he realized that he had no idea where Nigel was. And where, for that matter, was George the Racing President? All the worries that had left his mind when he found Oliver and the hat came swarming back. Were they still back in the present day, in the river? Or were they in 1776, with Sam?

The boat, by this point, was pulling up to shore, and George quickly disembarked and began issuing orders. Sam and Oliver followed the men from the boat, and Oliver sneezed all over Sam again. Sam was less pleased this time.

"Hey, can't you put your elbow over your face if you're going to do that?" he asked. But Oliver wasn't paying attention.

"Look!" he whispered, his voice having completely deserted him by this point. "There's George!"

"I know," Sam said impatiently. "We've been in the boat with him for hours now!"

"No," Oliver whispered loudly. "It's the other George! The Racing President! From the Nationals! What's he doing here?"

Sam looked. Indeed, the massive mascot was emerging

slowly from another boat. Nigel, who was looking around, still seemingly in shock, was beside him. Thank goodness! Sam was so glad to see his cousin, he started jumping up and down. He ran down the shore toward Nigel and leaped into his arms. Nigel hugged him back. Both of them were wet and shivering, but that didn't even matter.

"What is that?" a man cried from somewhere near Sam. The man was pointing at the Racing President, astonishment on his face. "What sort of apparition is it?"

"We shall take that along to fight the British!" another man said. "It will scare the daylights out of them!"

"It resembles the general!" a third man said.

"It is the general!" Oliver, who had followed Sam, whispered loudly to the third man. "It's George, the Racing President!"

"What does the boy say?" the second man said to the third man.

"He says it is George, the Racing President!" the third man said, sounding puzzled. "But we have no president. And why would he be racing?"

Meanwhile, the mascot was heading directly toward the real George. Maybe it wanted to meet its real-life counterpart, Sam thought, as he, Nigel, and Oliver followed behind the mascot.

"And what have we here?" George inquired, as the mascot approached him. "Sam, does this have something to do with you?" His voice sounded stern, but Sam could sense that he was trying not to laugh.

"Yes, sir," Sam said. "This is a special figure designed to honor you." The mascot nodded its head up and down.

"Fascinating," George said. "You always bring such interesting things into my life, Sam."

"Why, thank you, sir," Sam said, feeling extremely pleased. "As you do into mine."

George nodded back at the mascot, smiling, and the two exchanged a handshake.

Nigel, as if by habit, reached into his pocket for his cell phone, but it wasn't there. "I would have loved to get a picture of this," he exclaimed. "But my phone must have fallen out. Besides, it would have been ruined in the water." He leaned over toward Sam. "Would you be able to introduce me?" he asked, and gestured at George. The real one.

"Of course," Sam said. "General Washington, I would like to present my cousin, Nigel. He's from London, but he's a big admirer of yours."

George graciously extended his hand to Nigel. "Yes,

even in London, there are some who support our cause."

Nigel shook George's hand. "A pleasure, sir. And one day, there will be a university named for you, in a city named for you. And students like me will be attending it." He seemed, Sam noticed with approval, to know not to mention that he actually was attending such a school, in such a city. It would only confuse George, after all.

"Hmmm," George said thoughtfully. "Well, that would be nice."

At that moment, Oliver began sneezing again, over and over, and Sam was reminded that he needed to get Oliver back home. He wasn't sure whether the magic was stopping present-day time or not, especially as this adventure had unfolded outside the usual rules. He hated to leave George, but the play was that night, so time was of the essence. Surely he would get to see George again?

A couple of George's underlings rushed over at that point to consult with him, drawing him over toward one of the boats, and the hat seemed to twitch on Sam's head.

"Yes, we do need to leave," Sam said. "Is there any way you could get George the mascot back to Nationals Park in the present time and the rest of us back to my house, also in the present time?"

The hat bounced up and down. "Oh, yes, I need to take you off, that's right," Sam said, and he did. Then the swirling feeling descended and a moment later, Sam, the hat, Oliver, and Nigel were in Sam's front yard.

Cassie was walking down the street. "I tried calling,

but I got the voice mail," she said. "So I thought I'd come by and drag you home, Oliver."

Oliver, looking shell-shocked, nodded at his sister. "I have laryngitis," he whispered. "I can't talk at all." And he sneezed again.

"You poor thing!" she said. "Let's get you home right away. And why are you all wet?" And they headed up the street and around the corner, Oliver dragging behind his sister.

It was 5:45, an hour before Sam needed to be back at school for the play. He heaved a huge sigh of relief as he and Nigel entered the house.

Nigel reached into his pocket. "My phone! It's still here!" He tested it. "And it works, too!" He darted down to the basement, no doubt to call Celia.

"Well, I never!" the hat said. "Such a workout you've given me! I am completely drained! I am completely exhausted! All those extra wishes! Transferring some magic onto that statue! And of course that stone hat got the timing all wrong. The mascot wasn't much better, but at least it figured out to go into the water! I would have thought that was rather obvious!" And it gave Sam a meaningful look.

"Thank you so much," Sam said, overcome with thinking about all the efforts the hat had gone through. "Yes, I probably should have thought to go into the water, but I just didn't."

"Well, it's all right," the hat said. Its squeaky voice did sound tired. "But my dear Sam, I think our adventures might be at an end. My magic powers really are drained.

Today did take a lot out of me. Long-distance wishes, you know. Across time and space."

"Drained?" Sam said, a dull ache in his stomach. "You mean, forever?"

"I never say forever," the hat said. "I say for now." And it began snoring softly on Sam's lap.

Sam once again felt like crying. He hadn't had a chance to say goodbye to George. There were so many things he still wanted to ask him about! And—and now he'd just be a regular kid, with no magic adventures to look forward to.

The door opened, and Sam's parents came in, and soon they had all eaten dinner, Sam was back in his costume—including the hat, which was quiet—and they were in the car driving over to Eastview. Nigel, in the back seat with Sam, poked him and gestured that he should read something on his phone.

It was a link Celia had sent, to an article headlined "Missing 'George' Mascot Found," and it described a panicked situation at Nationals Park that afternoon when George the Racing President was nowhere to be found for approximately one hour, only to stroll in through the main gates, soaking wet.

Sam smiled. As they reached the school, Sam's parents and Nigel headed to the auditorium while Sam went to his classroom. He was one of the first ones there, and Ms. Martin pulled him aside, a worried look on her face.

"Sam, I've just heard from Oliver's parents," she said. "Apparently he's caught a terrible cold and has no voice left at all, and he's going to have to miss the play tonight."

A guilty feeling stole over Sam. If he hadn't brought Oliver along, Oliver wouldn't have gotten sick and wouldn't have missed the play. But then again, Sam hadn't forced Oliver to come. It had just sort of worked out that way. Still, he felt sad for Oliver, who was irritating but not a bad kid, when you stopped and thought about it.

"So, Sam, could you?" Ms. Martin was saying. Uh-oh, Sam thought. I have no idea what she's asking me to do. I wasn't paying attention again.

"I really think you're the only one in the class who can play the part," she was continuing. "You seem to know so much about George Washington, and I know it's a lot to ask at the last minute, but otherwise we're going to have to cancel our class's part of the show."

"Could I play George?" Sam asked. "Is that what you're asking?"

"Well, yes," said Ms. Martin, looking a little puzzled. "That's what I'm asking."

"Of course!" Sam said, a ripple of sheer delight coursing through him. "Yes! I would love to play George!" On his head, the hat, apparently awake again, was bouncing up and down.

"We really don't have time to rehearse," Ms. Martin said, her brow slightly furrowed. "You're just going to have to improvise."

"Oh, that's okay," Sam said. "I can do that."

By this point, the whole class was there, and it was time for the play to begin. Ms. Martin barely had time to explain the change of plans before it was time for Sam, as George, to take the stage.

It was as if the magic had returned, if briefly, because Sam could sense a buzzing coming from the hat on his head, and he could see George there, or a shadowy outline of George, standing over to one side of the stage. And as Sam reeled off the lines he had heard Oliver say and had heard George say, with a little improvisation of his own thrown in, Sam could see George smiling fondly.

The other cast members came in and out, playing their parts, and Sam kept going, and all of a sudden they had made it from the Revolutionary War to the White House, and then George had retired from the presidency and was heading to Mount Vernon, and then the play was over. Sam looked over to where George was standing and tipped his hat. George tipped his own hat to Sam, and then George slowly faded away. Sam kept staring over to the side where George had been, transfixed. Was that the last time he'd see George? He couldn't bear the thought of never seeing him again. He really had become a good friend, just as he'd told George the other day. And it was hard to stop seeing a friend, as Sam well knew.

"Sam!" Samantha was nudging him in the back. "Take a bow! They're all cheering for you!"

And sure enough, the whole auditorium was standing up and applauding, and Sam could see his parents and Nigel beaming at him from the third row. Sam took a bow, and Ms. Martin came up on stage and gave him a huge hug, and all his classmates were cheering too.

Eventually the clapping died down, and Sam's class left the stage so the other classes could have their turn.

"Oh, Sam, that was wonderful," Ms. Martin said backstage, her eyes misty. "I don't know how you captured his essence so well, and on such short notice, but thank you. We couldn't have done the play without you."

"You're welcome," Sam said, feeling misty himself.

"Great job, Sam!" Ava said, popping up by his side.

"Yeah," Samantha, as always, chimed in. "How did you do that without any rehearsing? That was incredible!"

"I'm not sure," Sam said, not knowing what else to say.

Just then, Andrew approached, and Ava and Samantha wandered off—although they remained close enough to listen if they had wanted to.

"Wow, Sam!" Andrew said, sounding sort of the way he used to after Sam had performed in a play, that special kind of congratulations that only a best friend can offer. "I mean, it really was like George himself was up on that stage!"

"Maybe he was," Sam said, smiling at Andrew.

"Yeah, maybe," Andrew said, grinning back at him. "Hey, maybe this weekend we could shoot a few baskets? I have baseball practice both days, but I do have some free time."

"Sure," Sam said. "I'd like that." And he could sense the hat, up on his head, nodding its approval.

As Sam went home that night, still all excited from the evening, and got into bed, he reflected on the past week. The hat was quietly resting on the chair next to Sam's bed, and Sam wasn't sure whether the magic really was gone, or just temporarily depleted. He wasn't sure whether he and Andrew would ever be able to recapture their old friendship or whether it would take another, lesser, form. He wasn't sure about a lot of things. But he did know that in the end, he would be okay even without the magic, and even without having Andrew as his best friend. That was something he'd learned from spending time with George. There was enough strength inside himself to manage perfectly well, even if he never had another magic adventure again.

But he certainly hoped he would!

Acknowledgments

In the course of writing this book, I read many books about George Washington, both for children and adults. To mention just a few that have stuck with me for years: the classic *George Washington* picture book by Ingri and Edgar Parin d'Aulaire, and Jean Fritz's books, particularly *George Washington's Mother* and *George Washington's Breakfast*.

Thank you to the helpful staff at Washington Crossing State Park in New Jersey, and Federal Hall National Memorial in New York, for kindly answering numerous questions over the phone.

I am so fortunate to have had the pleasure of working with the extremely talented Robert Lunsford, who created the amazing illustrations for this book. He and his equally wonderful wife, Kathleen, are some of my oldest friends. I was also incredibly lucky to meet Diane Nine many years ago. A good friend and a fantastic agent, she went above and beyond to find the perfect home for this book, and I am very appreciative. My gratitude also goes to Cheryl Weber for her careful editing and the team at Schiffer for embracing the book. Most important, I am grateful for my family. My mother Madeleine Kalb, a meticulous writer and editor, first suggested that I write a children's book about presidents. My father, Marvin Kalb, writer and journalist extraordinaire, has always set an incomparable standard. My husband, David Levitt, has displayed admirable patience, tolerance, and technological support through all of my writing and editing projects. My son, Aaron Kalb Levitt, the first one to read this book, is a source of joy and delight. And thanks to my sister and brother-in-law, Judith Kalb and Alex Ogden, and my niece, Eloise Rose Kalb Ogden. I love you all very much!

About the Author

Deborah Kalb is a freelance writer and editor who spent more than twenty years working as a journalist. She is the co-author, with her father, Marvin Kalb, of *Haunting Legacy: Vietnam and the American Presidency from Ford to Obama*, and has always been interested in presidents and history. She lives with her family in the Washington, DC, area.

About the Illustrator

Robert Lunsford has been a graphic artist/illustrator for nearly forty years. A graduate of Virginia Commonwealth University's School of the Arts, Rob spent his career as a graphic artist for his hometown daily newspaper, *The Roanoke Times*. Rob is known for his ability to tell stories through pictures and information graphics and is recognized by the Virginia Press Association, Society of News Design, and American Advertising Federation. A founding member and tuba/saxophone player in Roanoke's Norman Fishing Tackle Choir marching band, Rob enjoys woodworking, music, building things, and making pictures. He is married to a fellow artist and elementary school teacher and has two grown children.